## "Neither one of us is interested in a one-night stand."

At Dusty's words, Mimi held her breath. Did he care for her? Even half as much as she loved him?

"I'm proposing an exclusive semipermanent relationship that will provide us both with what we want. My attorney will draw up the papers—it'll all be perfectly legal." Dusty looked very pleased with himself.

"Let me see if I understand this," Mimi said carefully. "I give you sex—and take care of the baby. Anything else?"

He shifted uneasily. "Those are the highlights."

She nodded. "And in return, you'll give me...?"

"Whatever you want—cars, travel, your son's education. I want you in my life—"

"Not to mention in your bed."

"Damn right! My life *and* my bed. What else do you want?"

She tightened her lips and stared at him for a full minute, until he was squirming. Then she said one word: *"Marriage."*

While writing, **Ruth Jean Dale** often baby-sits her grandson. Being a completely impartial grandmother, she has concluded that he is the cutest, the smartest, the sweetest, the most adorable baby boy in the whole wide world and deserves to be immortalized. So she plotted *A Million Reasons Why*, in which the heroine falls in love with the cutest, the smartest, the sweetest, the most adorable baby boy—a replica of you-know-who! Baby Danny is also the catalyst for bringing together the hero and heroine.

Ruth and her family have recently moved from California to Colorado, and she loves it already. She's hoping to be snowbound so that she can hide herself away and write! Don't miss her Harlequin Romance novel, *Fireworks!*, available in July 1992.

## Books by Ruth Jean Dale

HARLEQUIN TEMPTATION
244—EXTRA! EXTRA!
286—TOGETHER AGAIN
315—ONE MORE CHANCE

EC A
G

# A Million Reasons Why

## RUTH JEAN DALE

# Harlequin Books

TORONTO • NEW YORK • LONDON
AMSTERDAM • PARIS • SYDNEY • HAMBURG
STOCKHOLM • ATHENS • TOKYO • MILAN

To Danny,
who graciously offered himself for baby research.
If I'd made the fictional Danny
half as cute, smart and adorable,
no one would ever believe it.
(And I'm not prejudiced, either!)
With love from Grandma.

Published January 1992

ISBN 0-373-25480-6

A MILLION REASONS WHY

# Prologue

THE CHECK TURNED OUT to be just a bit less than Mimi
Carlton had expected—about two hundred and fifty
thousand dollars less. Convinced her eyes were playing
tricks, she blinked and looked again.

The numbers leaped out at her: eight hundred and
thirty-seven dollars and sixty-seven cents. Her stomach
clenched; not much to show as settlement for her late
husband's estate. Profoundly shocked, she felt the world
as she knew it spin off its axis.

David's former business partner slipped an arm
around her waist and led her away. "Don't worry, babe,"
he whispered into her ear. "Good-looker like you—I'll
think of something to keep you off the streets." He
snickered.

What he eventually thought of was illegal in seventeen states and the District of Columbia, but at least it
managed to shock Mimi out of her stupor. He was
brushing spaghetti off his lap and sputtering impreca-
tions when she stormed out of Mama Mia's Pizzeria.

As she unlocked the front door of the modest Denver
home she could no longer afford, the telephone rang. She
answered against her better judgment and heard a snippy
voice announce that eleven-year-old J.D. was being ex-
pelled, a mere two days before Christmas vacation was
to begin.

It seemed authorities had finally figured out who broke into the school computer and programmed it to give all the boys *A*'s and all the girls *F*'s. Except for Suzy Miller. J.D. liked Suzy Miller. Suzy got triple *A*'s.

Mimi trekked through a Colorado snowstorm to retrieve her precocious offspring, too numb to offer more than a token tongue-lashing. The latest escapade by her freckle-faced string bean of a son was merely one more straw on the back of her already overburdened camel.

It took a shockingly short time to throw their meager personal possessions into suitcases and cardboard boxes. J.D., perhaps figuring he'd pushed his luck far enough for one day, seemed to take their hasty departure from the only home he'd ever known with perfect assurance. He didn't even bat an eye when they checked into the Trail's End Inn. While Mimi sat on the edge of one double bed and tried to think straight, the boy prowled around his newly shrunken universe.

"Hey, neat!" he yelled from the bathroom door. "Little bars of soap and glasses wrapped in paper. All right!"

"J.D.," Mimi said, "we've got to talk."

"Sure, Mom."

He trotted past her to yank open the top drawer in the small, wall-mounted desk. The room, decorated in a sort of Early Mountain Dingy, featured faded paper murals of old prospectors and scraggy burros.

J.D. pulled out several sheets of stationery and waved them in the air. "Hey, I can write to Aunt Gloria," he announced.

"J.D., please come sit down here and listen to me." Mimi patted the desert-colored bedspread.

"Go ahead and talk. I can hear okay."

J.D. closed one drawer and opened the next, keeping his back toward his mother. His voice sounded suddenly guarded, and she saw tension in the stiff set of his narrow shoulders. With a sinking heart, she realized she wasn't the only one who was frightened.

That knowledge unnerved her. She wasn't accustomed to glimpsing J.D.'s vulnerabilities. With a sky-high IQ and an eleven-going-on-forty outlook, he rarely reacted like the kid he was. His father's illness and death had ended J.D.'s childhood too soon.

She took a deep breath and tried to speak with assurance. "Your father's estate was finally settled today."

J.D. darted her a quick glance over one hunched shoulder. "I figured." He hesitated. "We broke?"

"N-not exactly." She couldn't meet his skeptical look. "Well, almost."

He let out his breath in an exasperated sigh. "I told Pop to put his bucks in mutual funds, but would he listen?" He closed the drawer and turned, his young face blank. "How bad is it?"

"Pretty bad." She fished in her shirt pocket for the check and held it out.

He read the numbers and his eyes widened. "Bummer!"

"My sentiments exactly."

"What about the house?"

"Your father's partner holds the mortgage on it."

J.D.'s lip curled. "That slime wad?"

For once she didn't chastise him for that characterization. "The same."

"He threw us out?"

"Something like that."

His mouth tightened and he thrust out his chin. "What about the Casa de Carlos?"

"Our share went toward the medical bills." Mimi resisted an urge to bury her face in her hands. This was no time to give in to self-pity. "And taxes. And debts. Oh, J.D., there's no point talking about it. Everything's gone."

"Wow!" His eyes grew round in amazement. "We're statistics!"

"What?"

"You know, homeless. I read a story in the newspaper the other day, how all these down-on-their-luck people live on the streets and sleep in cardboard boxes...."

Horrified, she stared at him. "We are *not* going to sleep on the streets!"

"I guess it is pretty cold. If it was summer..." He crossed to the bed and sat down warily, at least two feet from her. He didn't like to be touched and was obviously taking no chances that she'd grab him or do some other motherly thing. "I'll get a job," he announced with sudden determination.

"Doing what? You're eleven years old!"

His face fell. "Oh, yeah." He perked up again. "Maybe I could tutor?"

"Maybe," she agreed doubtfully. "Tough, though, when you've been kicked out of school."

"Oh, yeah." He screwed up his face in thought. "I could get a paper route."

"J.D., you don't even own a bicycle anymore!"

He glared at her. "You think of something, then."

She sighed. "I'll start looking for a job tomorrow. Cook, waitress, hostess... I don't know how to do much of anything else." Galling thought, but her work experience was limited. Worse—she hadn't much liked the restaurant business to begin with, although David had loved it. Now it looked as if she'd be stuck in it forever.

When they had opened the Casa de Carlos Mexican Restaurant, it had been the culmination of his dream, not hers. He'd promised she wouldn't need to work there once they got the place on its financial feet. He'd tried to keep that pledge, but some emergency had always come up—last and worst, the brain tumor that had killed him a year ago, after a long, hellish decline.

He'd taken in a partner along the way, explaining to Mimi that they needed the money, but they also needed the help. *David, if you only knew!*

"Where we gonna live, if the street's out?"

Mimi blinked in surprise. "Why..."

She'd just assumed they'd find an apartment and stay in Denver, but why should they? They had a few friends, but no family in Colorado. She didn't much care for the weather, and J.D. was persona non grata with the school system.

"Where would you like to live?" she asked.

He frowned. "The way I figure it, there's Aunt Gloria in California or Uncle George in Missouri."

"Which would you prefer?"

He pursed his lips. "Aunt Gloria's, I guess." He hesitated. "I didn't much like that guy who came to see you when we visited Uncle George after... after Dad..."

Mimi nodded quickly, knowing he didn't want to use the word "died" in connection with his father. "Why not? Clint Conover is a very nice man. I went to school with him—what's not to like?"

J.D. shrugged. "He tried to make brownie points with me."

"Why on earth would Clint Conover want to make brownie points with a kid, no offense?"

"To get to you, Mom. Wake up and smell the roses, why don't you? Jeez!" J.D. sprang to his feet. "He really laid it on. Told me how you were the 'purtiest little ol' gal who ever come outta Granby, Ma-zur-ah.' He said you could'a had any man you wanted but 'she picked yore daddy.'" He exaggerated the accent. "Sheesh!"

"Well, what do you know." The thought that Clint still found her attractive brought a warming glow to Mimi's numb interior. It also reminded her of something she'd all but forgotten.

She still had her looks. Maybe she should do something with them while she had time.

Assuming she did. It'd been such a hellacious day, she might have aged ten years during the course of it. She lifted her right hand to her cheek, seeking reassurance.

"Excuse me," she said abruptly to her son. She rose from the bed, hurried into the bathroom and closed the door. For a moment she stood there in the dark, her eyes squeezed shut. She had never felt so alone . . . or so frightened.

Switching on the strong fluorescent lighting, she leaned forward to study her reflection in the slightly clouded mirror. Starting at the top of her head, she examined herself with brutal detachment.

A cap of thick, strawberry-blond curls cascaded over her forehead, the color perhaps not as vivid as it had once been, but not bad. And the curl was natural. Yes, the hair was a definite plus.

She'd longed for a classic, oval face instead of the one she had: heart-shaped, with high cheekbones and a firm little chin. Her skin had always been her best feature, and she saw that it still was . . . smooth and fine-textured, with the tinge of ripe peaches in her cheeks. Not a freckle in sight, she was pleased to note.

Her skin was looking a little dry, though. She'd been taking it for granted, a dangerous oversight in the dead of a Colorado winter.

Natural darker brows framed misty-brown eyes fringed with thick, curling lashes. She leaned closer, looking for telltale signs of age...and found them. A few faint lines fanned out from the corners of her eyes, a portent of things to come.

She turned her head sideways and peered over one shoulder while she traced the straight line of her nose with a forefinger. With her other hand she patted up beneath her chin—only one, thank heaven.

Leaning closer to the mirror again, she tried an experimental smile. Her teeth were straight and white, the result of good genes rather than good dentistry. Her mouth she considered a bit generous, but not too bad.

A banging on the bathroom door made her jump.

"Hey, you fall in or something?" J.D. yelled from the other side. "I've got a surprise. Come on out, okay?"

She opened the bathroom door and the first thing she saw was the brave flame of a small candle. It was anchored in a snack cake that looked like a blob of marshmallow rolled in coconut tinted an outrageous pink.

The whole was offered proudly by a very pleased young man. "Happy birthday, Mom," J.D. said with a big grin. "I'll bet you thought I forgot."

Quick tears leaped into Mimi's thirty-nine-year-old eyes and she swallowed hard. "Oh, John David," she murmured. "How did you manage...?"

He shrugged. "Nothin' to it. Make a wish and blow out your candle, okay?"

"Okay." She bit her lip. She had a birthday wish coming; surely this was a good omen. What did she most desire in all the world?

Love? No, not love. She'd had love and lost it, and couldn't imagine she'd be lucky enough to find it again. What, then?

Security and companionship. That was what she wanted—no, required. She'd worked and struggled for so long. Now she needed help, she realized, help in paying the bills, in raising J.D., in making all the millions of decisions that threatened her sanity.

As she gazed at the steady golden flame, a wish born of desperation formed in her mind: *By the time I'm forty, I want to marry a rich man.*

She blinked against the prickle of tears and blew mightily. The flame flickered and died. Mimi began to laugh, because it was better than crying.

"Mom, you okay?"

She pulled herself together. "Never better," she said. "J.D., we're not licked. We've got eight hundred thirty-seven dollars and sixty-seven cents."

"Yeah?"

Mimi grinned. "Want to go out to dinner?"

# 1

THE KITCHEN SMELLED of Christmas—cinnamon and vanilla, the yeasty goodness of baking bread, and undertones of pine. Mimi surveyed the racks of cooling cookies in holiday shapes, smiling at her handiwork.

"Whatcha doin', hon?" Gloria asked from the doorway.

"Just being happy," Mimi said softly. She glanced at her sister with love and gratitude.

A strong family resemblance proclaimed the relationship, but the similarity was more in bone structure than anything else. Gloria Van Husen, older by three years, was taller and thinner and lacked her sister's natural beauty. Years ago she'd learned to compensate with cosmetics and clothes that gave her an air of sophistication to which Mimi had never aspired.

Twice divorced and once widowed, Gloria lived alone in an enormous and expensive house overlooking the Westbrook Country Club in Southern California. When her sister and nephew showed up on her doorstep only a few days before Christmas, Gloria had welcomed them with open arms.

Now she walked into her spacious kitchen, gold bracelets jingling on one thin, salon-tanned wrist. "Never did take much to please you," she teased. "I keep telling you, set your sights higher."

Mimi picked up a hot pad and leaned down to open the oven door. "Little do you know," she muttered, tapping the brown crust of a loaf of baking bread. At the hollow thunk, she removed two bread pans from the oven and set them on the tiled counter.

Gloria crossed to the drip coffee maker. "Come sit down and let's talk," she ordered. She filled two cups and carried them to the breakfast bar, where she slid onto a stool.

"Let me clean up a little first," Mimi suggested.

"Leave it for Lupe."

"But—"

"It's her job, Mimi." Gloria looked at her sister, one brow arching. "I pay her to take care of things. You want her out of work on Christmas Eve?"

Mimi couldn't think of an argument to beat that. She piled cookies onto a small plate and brought them to the breakfast bar. "It just doesn't seem right somehow," she grumbled, sitting down.

Gloria shook her head, smiling. "You're the limit, girl." Her shrewd gaze narrowed. "So tell me."

"Tell you what?" Mimi hedged.

Gloria gave an exasperated snort. "Everything! I've been patient—haven't I been patient?"

Mimi conceded that point with a shrug. "So?"

"So I know you—you're up to something. What is it?"

Mimi picked up a star-shaped cookie and broke off one golden point. "It's silly."

"Mimi!" Gloria fixed her sister with a mock-threatening gaze.

"Oh, all right." Mimi popped the bit of cookie into her mouth. "It's just that...the day everything fell apart was my birthday." She looked up suddenly. "Gloria, do you know any rich guys? My birthday wish was to marry one."

Gloria's jaw dropped and her brown eyes widened. "You mean it?"

Mimi sighed. "I did at the time. J.D. and I ... we both need a man in our lives. There's a million reasons why, but a little financial security is close to the top of the list."

Gloria beamed. "You've come to your senses!"

"You think so?" Mimi's tone was doubtful.

"Sure. Haven't I always told you it's as easy to love a rich man as a poor man?"

"Yes, but I never believed you."

"That's because you were so young when you hooked up with David, and he was so poor. You never gave yourself a chance."

"I loved him," Mimi declared with dignity.

"Of course you did. You'd have to love a man to go through ..."

Gloria's voice trailed away; Mimi knew neither of them wanted to remember the last two years of her husband's life.

Mimi swallowed. "Then you don't think I'm being ... completely gross and mercenary?"

"Good Lord, no. For once in your life you're showing some sense." Gloria's eyes narrowed, as if she sensed Mimi's uncertainty. "Besides, you should be thinking of J.D. He needs a daddy as much as you need a husband."

"Yes." Mimi knew that at the moment J.D. was outside, following the gardener around. The boy hungered for the attentions of a man, a man who wasn't sick or frightened or worried to death. It hurt to remember what had happened to David, but it hurt almost as much to see J.D.'s need. She'd always believed fiercely that the welfare of children must always come first, yet had found herself powerless to protect her son.

"So what's your plan?" Gloria demanded.

Mimi sighed. "Who plans? I just thought I'd look for a job where rich men congregate."

"Spontaneous as always, I see." Drumming painted porcelain nails on the countertop, Gloria gave her sister an assessing look. "Why get any job at all?"

"We've got to live, Glo. You know my financial situation."

Gloria nodded. "But do you know mine? Look at this place." She made a sweeping gesture with one arm. "I'm loaded, girl. I'm also alone—no husband, no children. Unlike you, I'm not eager to get seriously entangled with another man, but I sure like the idea of having my favorite sister and my favorite nephew around."

Warm gratitude flooded through Mimi. "I'm your only sister, and J.D.'s your only nephew," she observed, her voice a bit thick.

"A mere detail," Gloria scoffed. "What I'm getting at is, you don't have to work. I'll back you—you just go on a manhunt. Believe me, it's easier to marry money if you've already *got* money, or at least appear to."

"That's dishonest."

Gloria shifted impatiently on her stool. "You know what they say—fake it till you make it. Besides, the question will never come up. Trust me."

Mimi supposed she had no choice if this was going to work. And she wanted it to work, although she still felt uncomfortable about her goal. She was tired of worrying about every dime. She wanted J.D. to have the advantages she couldn't afford, especially a good—which meant expensive—education.

Last, but not least, she simply wanted a man in her life. Maybe Gloria could live alone; Mimi wasn't interested in trying.

But she wouldn't let Gloria pick up the tab. "I appreciate the offer, but I'll feel better working," she said. "I was thinking you might know someone at the country club. That should be a good place to meet men with money."

"That's the place," Gloria agreed, "and the time is New Year's Eve. I've got a date and you're coming along. That'll pretty much give you a chance to look over the field all at once."

"I don't want to be a fifth wheel."

Gloria shushed her. "I can think of three men, offhand, who might do. All three are loaded, all three are members of the country club, and two out of the three are passable in the looks department."

"And the third?"

A small smile curved Gloria's mouth and her eyelids drooped. "The third is in a class all by himself. Dustin McLain..." She sighed. "Let's just say Dusty could eat crackers in my bed anytime."

That got Mimi's attention. "Tell me more."

Gloria smiled. "I'll let you find out for yourself on New Year's Eve," she said mysteriously.

And that was all she'd say, even though Mimi teased, cajoled and nagged right up to the last minute.

SHE WAS PUTTING the finishing touches on her makeup New Year's Eve, anticipating the evening ahead, when J.D. sauntered into the bedroom.

"Where you goin'?" he demanded, a frown on his freckled face.

Mimi's eyes met those of her son's in the mirror. "I told you, honey. Aunt Gloria and I are going to a New Year's Eve party at the country club."

J.D. nodded. "You got a date?" he demanded, his tone sharply critical.

"No, but Aunt Gloria does. I'm just tagging along."

He nodded again. He'd asked the same questions twice already and he seemed reassured by her answers.

"But," she forced herself to add, "that's not to say I'll never have a date. You understand that, right?"

He nodded. "Sure. Just not yet." He turned to go.

"J.D.?"

He gave her a questioning look.

"Are you happy here, honey?"

He shrugged. "Sure. Why not?"

"I'm afraid Christmas wasn't—"

"Christmas was fine, Mom," he interrupted. "I don't need a lot of junk. The stamps you gave me for my collection and the bike from Aunt Gloria—that was plenty."

It didn't feel like plenty to her, but she was grateful for his reassurance. "John David Carlton," she said softly, "I love you."

"Yeah, well." He squinched up his face and turned away. "You look good," he said gruffly as he passed through the doorway, hunching his shoulders as if embarrassed.

She smiled after him for a moment and then turned to the mirror. A stranger stared back.

She'd applied a more dramatic makeup than usual, heeding her sister's exhortation to go for sophistication. Borrowed diamonds sparkled at her throat. The glittery peacock-blue gown, a Christmas gift from Gloria, clung in all the right places and made Mimi's own coloring all the more vivid.

"Remember, you're a woman of the world," Gloria had stressed. "You and I may kid around with Missouri down-home folksiness when we're by ourselves, but that's not the bait you need on this fishing trip. No talk about the simple joys of baking cookies or the wonders of picking oranges off the trees in the backyard. And for goodness' sake, hold off telling anyone about J.D. You don't look old enough to have an eleven-year-old kid. Don't spoil the illusion."

Mimi fervently hoped her sister was right. Looking at her reflection in the mirror, she sighed. This was getting complicated, when she wanted it to be simple. She wanted to walk into the country club and see a gorgeous man across the room. Their eyes would meet and it would be love at first sight.

Naturally he would be rich and love children. Before the evening was over, he'd sweep her into his arms and kiss her silly.

That presented a minor problem; she hadn't been kissed in so long, she wasn't sure she remembered how. Was it like riding a bicycle? Did you ever forget?

In her daydreams she remembered, all right. One touch of her ruby lips and the guy'd be putty in her hands. "Come with me to the Casbah," he'd say. *Wait a minute, wrong fantasy!*

Mimi laughed and gave her high-piled curls a final pat. Optimism flooded through her. She could do sophistication; sure she could.


THE WESTBROOK Country Club sparkled with Christmas lights. Even the stately grouping of palm trees at the front entrance had been decorated. Enchanted, Mimi stared at this wonderland through the window of Neil Gordon's two-year-old Ford. She simply couldn't get used to the idea of Christmas and New Year's without snow and cold. Not even Gloria's indulgent smile could quell Mimi's sense of excitement.

The car moved sedately up the curving driveway and stopped. Uniformed parking attendants sprang forward, whisked open the doors, and the three alighted.

"After you, ladies." Neil bowed slightly and gestured the two women forward. His bald head gleamed in the artificial light.

According to Gloria, she and Neil were just friends and would never be more. Mimi wasn't so sure. He was really quite a nice man and devoted to her sister, although neither socially nor economically up to Gloria's usual standards.

Gloria shivered and drew her mink more closely around her shoulders. "This weather is just terrible," she complained. "Usually December's one of our nicest months."

Mimi wanted to laugh; the breeze seemed downright balmy compared to what she'd left behind. She'd accepted the loan of a velvet evening coat only at Gloria's insistence.

"The cold doesn't seem to be bothering your baby sister any, sugar," Neil declared. "Mimi, where'd you say you came in from?"

Mimi, leading the way toward heavy glass doors held open by an attendant, glanced back. "Denver. When I headed west, snow was a foot deep and—"

Something brushed against her arm and she stopped short, instantly aware that she'd violated another's space. Swinging around with words of apology forming on her lips, she lifted her gaze and connected with eyes that couldn't possibly be as clear and blue as they seemed.

She had never looked upon a more ruggedly handsome face in her life. She had a quick impression of cleanly etched features that radiated strength, of a classically molded mouth that did not smile, yet wasn't unfriendly.

She swallowed hard and tried to speak. "I beg your pardon. I . . . I . . ."

He nodded, his grave expression unchanging. She found herself thinking that when this man smiled, he would mean it.

"My fault entirely, ma'am. Are you all right?"

She heard the laconic drawl that bespoke wide-open spaces and Western chivalry. His tone seemed at odds with, yet curiously right for, the sophistication of his classic black tuxedo.

He'd asked her a question; she saw his dark brows rise in inquiry. Feeling like a complete and utter fool, she gave her sister a glance that begged *help me!* Gloria smiled serenely.

"Good evening, Dustin. I hoped we'd run into you tonight, but not literally. This is my sister, Mimi Carlton. Mimi, Dustin McLain."

Mimi all but groaned aloud. Gloria hadn't oversold this man one iota. What an inauspicious beginning! She offered her hand. "I usually watch where I'm going, Mr. McLain," she said a trifle breathlessly.

He took her hand into his with an authority that implied strength without insisting upon it. "Then you're one in a million," he said in the same slow drawl. "And call me Dusty."

"Dusty." She gave him a smile, trying to entice him into returning it. Somehow she suspected that a smile on that strong, immobile face would be . . . something to write home about.

"And this," he said, drawing someone forward, "is Carri Gibson."

Mimi felt as if she'd been hit over the head with a baseball bat. How could she possibly have been so stunned by this man's presence that she hadn't even noticed the woman at his side—his date?

Carri Gibson, blond and beautiful and thirtyish, smiled with impersonal aplomb. "So nice to see you all," she murmured. She slid one hand beneath her escort's arm. "Dusty, we're blocking the entrance. Don't you think we should go inside?"

Dusty patted her hand where it rested at the crook of his elbow. "Neil, ladies." He nodded and turned away. He still hadn't smiled; he hadn't been unfriendly, he simply hadn't smiled.

Mimi stood there thunderstruck and watched the couple disappear inside. *There went a man!*

Gloria touched Mimi's shoulder, urging her forward. "Good grief, girl," she whispered. "I figured the two of you would hit it off, but you look like you've just been poleaxed."

Mimi uttered a breathless little laugh. "Don't be ridiculous," she denied. "I was just surprised, that's all." But she couldn't help adding, "Lord, he's gorgeous."

"I warned you," Gloria said smugly. "Quit drooling, now. It's time to party!"

And party they did. Neil found a table in the rapidly filling ballroom, and soon they were surrounded by revelers bearing noisemakers and wearing paper party hats. A constant stream of men stopped by, and women, too.

Mimi wasn't surprised at this evidence of Gloria's popularity. Everyone liked Gloria; it had always been that way. She was open and nonjudgmental and fun to be with. Not for the first time, Mimi was proud to be her sister.

It soon became apparent, however, that not everyone was there simply to enjoy the pleasure of Gloria's wit and wisdom. Surrounded by attentive men, Mimi smiled at them all without favoritism, accepting champagne and invitations to dance.

Oh, she was having fun! It had been so long, so very long... since before David's brain tumor was diagnosed. She'd missed being admired, she'd missed flirting, and she'd especially missed male attention.

She felt for all the world like the Sleeping Beauty of fairy-tale fame. All she needed to make her evening complete was a kiss from a handsome prince.

Whirled around in the arms of a middle-aged gentleman, she laughed with pleasure as her glance flew across the room to collide with Dusty's. He stood on a mezzanine, Carri beside him, but as far as Mimi was concerned he was all alone. He looked straight at her, his expression slightly puzzled.

Her partner whisked her away. Although she twisted and strained to see the lanky figure, he was lost to her across the sea of New Year's revelers.

CARRI TUGGED IMPATIENTLY at Dusty's arm. "Dusty? Listen to me!"

Dusty forced his attention from the dance floor to the woman beside him. "I'm sorry. What did you say?"

"I said..." Her hazel eyes sparkled with anger. "Sometimes you make me so mad I could just...!" She clamped her lips together.

After a while he said, "I know." He let his gaze slide back over the dance floor, but the woman with the red-gold hair was gone.

Just as well.

Carri spoke through clenched jaws. "All right, I made a mistake. I admit it. I thought you'd be jealous, but instead you . . . you don't even seem to care."

"Sure I care." He spoke as gently as he could. "I care enough that I want us to part friends. That's the only reason I'm here tonight."

"Damn you! Not everyone's as perfect as you are! For once in your life, can't you give somebody a break?"

He gazed down at her face, a lovely face, really . . . but not special to him, even before he'd discovered her talent for stretching the truth. Still, he was reluctant to hurt her.

"Sweetheart," he said, choosing his words with care, "we never had a future. This just speeded things up."

"You don't ever intend to marry again, do you." It was a statement, not a question. "You're forty-two years old and the loneliest man I ever knew, but you don't ever intend to let another woman get really close to you."

He frowned. He didn't like being characterized as lonely. "I told you that from the beginning."

"But I didn't believe you!" She clenched her small hands into fists.

"And now you do." He cupped her chin with one hand and tilted her face toward his. "I tried marriage. I wasn't any good at it. If I had weakened, you'd have been too smart to say yes."

"Like hell I would! Why do you think I hung around for three years?"

Tears sparkled on her lashes and he looked away. He wanted to leave her with her dignity intact, but she wasn't making it easy. He always wanted to leave them with their dignity. He was beginning to think the only way to do that was to move into a cave and become a damned hermit.

Unfortunately, he enjoyed women much too much to try that. *Liar,* what he enjoyed was sex. Unfortunately, that was part of a package deal.

"Would you like me to take you home?" he asked after a moment.

She lifted her chin. "No. It's New Year's Eve. Out with the old, in with the new." She slid her arms around his neck, dragging his face down until it was close to hers. "I could have made you happy," she declared in an angry whisper, thrusting her hips against him.

"Maybe so." He didn't want to wound her with the truth. "But I don't have a single doubt that I'd have made you miserable." He disentangled her arms and turned her around until her back was against his chest.

She flashed a challenging glance over one bare shoulder. It was a wasted effort. He already understood that she would try to make him jealous. She should have understood that wasn't possible.

He gave the bottom in the tight black satin gown an impersonal pat. "Go get 'em, honey," he invited.

MIMI ADJUSTED the pink foil cone atop her curls. The party had been fun, but she wasn't used to such unrestrained merrymaking. She stifled a yawn and looked around at the happy throng.

Confetti and streamers sifted down from the mezzanine, from nets looped strategically below the crystal chandeliers. The noise level had climbed steadily, until now it was impossible to be heard without shouting.

"Champagne?"

Someone thrust a glass into Mimi's hand and she obediently lifted it to her lips. She'd paced her drinking and felt only a very slight, very pleasant, buzz.

Gloria, on the other hand, was feeling no pain. She'd long since switched from champagne—sissy drink, she called it—to vodka. Mimi shuddered as she watched her sister toss down the clear liquid like water.

A slightly slurred male voice interrupted her thoughts. "Happy New Year, Mimi!"

She turned and looked into the smiling face of Martin Montgomery, one of Gloria's three nominees for brother-in-law honors. There was nothing wrong with Martin, except that he was thirty-five, so Mimi considered him a shade too young. There was nothing particularly right about him, either. She found him attractive in a bland way, but he paled to insignificance beside . . .

"Happy New Year to you, too, Martin," she said quickly. She lifted her glass and sipped.

He waited until she had finished and then took the glass from her fingers. "That's no way to welcome in a new year," he scolded.

He caught her hand and drew her to her feet. *He's going to kiss me!* she realized, feeling a dart of panic at the prospect. As he leaned toward her, her glance skittered over his shoulder and came to rest upon the face of a lanky man leaning against the wall.

Dusty McLain's cool expression never altered as his gaze met Mimi's. Then her view of him was blotted out by Martin. She turned her head quickly and his lips grazed her cheek.

"Oh, look," she said brightly. "Gloria's leading the countdown."

"Nineteen . . . eighteen . . . seventeen . . ." Gloria stood on the mezzanine, a champagne flute containing straight vodka in one hand, a megaphone in the other. Neil stood nearby, frowning slightly. He was not among those urging her on.

Martin nuzzled the hair at Mimi's temples. "C'mon, Mimi." He sounded slightly tipsy.

"Please," she said quickly, stepping away, "can you find me another glass of champagne for the toast? It's almost midnight!"

"I suppose." He gave her a puzzled frown. Weaving slightly, he turned and was instantly swallowed up by the crowd.

Mimi sighed with relief. So much for her plan to marry a rich man. Even when she found one, she didn't know what to do with him.

" . . . six . . . wait a minute, where was I? Oh—nine . . ." Gloria's tone dared the New Year to put in an appearance before she was ready.

Mimi turned back toward the table, feeling alone even in the crowd. Hands settled on her shoulders and she tensed. Had Martin returned already? Her heart sank.

" . . . two . . . *one!*" Pandemonium exploded, along with a deafening rendition of "Auld Lang Syne." Balloons and confetti rained down upon her head, and the grip on her shoulders tightened.

"Happy New Year," a voice whispered into her ear with electric clarity, despite the general tumult—not Martin Montgomery's voice, but a drawl that tightened her scalp and sent shivers of anticipation rippling up her spine.

She turned slowly beneath the light grip, opening her eyes wide. Dusty stood there, wearing the same unruffled expression she had seen before. He cupped her chin with one hand and tilted up her face.

"Tradition demands," he said gravely, and leaned down.

It never even occurred to her to try to avoid his lips, as she had Martin's. Instead she rose on tiptoe and slipped her arms around his neck, turning her head so that their mouths met at a perfect angle.

The shock of that first touch took her breath away. She felt no awkwardness and no self-consciousness, only a soaring anticipation that was new and yet strangely familiar.

Their mouths fitted together like two halves of a perfect whole, and her lips parted beneath his at just the right moment. His tongue slid past her teeth, and new sensations of delight assailed her with each tender, probing stroke.

His hands tightened on her waist to draw her hard against his taut length. She arched her back, pressing her breasts against the solid strength of his chest, flexing her right knee slightly to insinuate it between the strong columns of his legs.

She felt giddy as if she were clinging to a roller coaster careening out of control. Her nipples tightened to a near-painful rigidity, and liquid warmth flooded through her. Her entire body responded to this stranger as if she'd been waiting for him, and him alone. It was a profoundly shocking revelation—shocking and exciting.

He lifted his head and the noisy celebration intruded instantly, reminding her that she stood in a public place, in the arms of a man with whom she'd never even had a real conversation.

Did the communion of souls count? she wondered with giddy confusion. The communion of bodies?

A paper spiral drifted down to join the glittering flecks of confetti in his dark hair. His expression remained as cool as ever, but his heart pounded beneath her palms, flattened against his chest.

He tugged gently on one strawberry-blond curl. "It will be," he said.

She blinked, effectively breaking the spell. Feeling suddenly uneasy, she stepped away from him, her movements jerky. "Will be what?" she asked, surprised how breathless she sounded.

"A Happy New Year. I have a feeling—"

Martin emerged from the crowd. "I made it!" he exclaimed. Champagne sloshed from the glass he carried, wetting his hand and leaving damp streaks on his tuxedo. "Happy New Year, Mimi!"

He leaned down and planted a kiss upon her mouth before she could recoil. His lips were too soft and too wet and she stiffened, remembering the firm, sensual pressure of Dusty's kiss. She gave Martin a shove and straightened away from him, but it was too late.

Dusty was gone, swallowed up by the roistering crowd.

# 2

GLORIA STUMBLED into the kitchen a few minutes past noon on the first day of the new year. Mimi and J.D., finishing a lunch of tuna salad sandwiches and tomato soup, exchanged knowing glances.

"Uh-oh," J.D. muttered. Standing up, he swigged the last of the milk in his glass. "I'm outta here."

Gloria watched him go, her lip curling. "Little pitchers have big ears," she croaked. She walked unsteadily to the breakfast bar and slumped onto a stool. "I'd have to get better to die."

"You poor thing," Mimi commiserated automatically. She gave her sister a cup of strong black coffee. "You really should eat something."

"I'd barf. Which I'll do anyway, if you don't get all sight and smell of tuna out of here."

Mimi cleared the table and then sat down again. The two maintained a morose silence, until at last Gloria groaned. "I feel like the last rose of summer," she announced.

"Me, too," Mimi agreed listlessly.

Gloria downed at least half the contents of her cup. "What's your problem, Snow White? I didn't exactly see you under the table last night—and if you'd been there, believe me, I'd have seen you."

"That's true. Gloria, I don't like to sound critical, but don't you think—?"

"Lecture me not, sister dear." Gloria held up one hand in a warning gesture. "If you want to be useful, relate amusing tales of the foibles of my friends. Kindly skip the part where I danced on the piano with a light shade on my head."

"But that was the best part," Mimi teased.

"No. The best part was when Dusty McLain planted a big one on you."

Mimi stared at her sister. "How did you know that?" she demanded, her heart lurching at the memory.

"I saw it, girl. I knew you'd like him. I just wasn't sure how he'd react to you. In the past, he's been . . . let's call it elusive."

"He still is." Mimi stared into her coffee cup. "Martin Montgomery interrupted us, and when I looked around, Dusty was gone. I guess he was simply doing what he said—observing a New Year's tradition."

"Ha!"

"He was there with another woman," Mimi pointed out, eschewing false hope.

"And she left with another guy."

"Really?" Was Dusty available? Could he have felt at least a tiny fraction of what *she*'d felt when they kissed? Even now she couldn't put a name to it; all she knew was that it had been powerful enough to linger through a sleepless night.

"Really," Gloria said emphatically. "He'd be perfect for you. He's loaded—land, a couple of shopping centers, I don't know what all." Her expression grew glum. "But I guess I should warn you that Dusty's a hard man to hook—and believe me, plenty have made the effort. It's worth a try, though, especially since . . ."

"Especially since what?" Mimi felt a plummeting sensation in the pit of her stomach.

Gloria pursed her lips and narrowed her eyes. "I talked to the manager of the country club last night. There's no way he's going to hire you."

"But when you introduced me he seemed so . . . so friendly and nice," Mimi protested, disappointed.

"Exactly. And so did every other man you met. That's the problem. He said he wouldn't dare hire you—the wives would have a fit."

"Why, of all the—!" Mimi couldn't think of words bad enough. "He—I—we—!"

The wall-mounted telephone rang.

Gloria groaned and covered her ears with her hands. "Get that, will you?" she pleaded. "It's probably Dusty, anyway."

"Right." Mimi made a disdainful face. "Or the manager of the country club offering me a job." She leaned over and lifted the receiver. "Van Husen residence."

A slight pause; the hair on the back of her neck prickled. Then a voice said her name like a question.

"Yes." She swallowed hard. "Hello, Dusty."

Gloria reeled back on her bar stool. "Gad," she muttered, "I'm clairvoyant!"

"I was wondering . . ." Dusty began.

Mimi heard reluctance in his tone and an unexpected shyness. How could a man with Dusty's looks and money possibly be shy? She must be imagining things. "Yes?" she said in an encouraging voice.

"Asking for a date at my age is ridiculous," he said, "but I don't know you well enough to call it anything else."

Her heart began to pound. "You're asking me for a date?"

Gloria's eyebrows climbed and she mouthed a single word: *"Wow!"*

"Mmm-hmm. I realize you don't know me, but I think your sister will vouch for me as a responsible citizen, last night notwithstanding."

Mimi glanced at the sister in question. Gloria was literally jumping up and down on her stool, her head bobbing *Yes*, before she even knew the question. "That wouldn't surprise me in the least," Mimi agreed.

"I thought you might like to go horseback riding, but on second thought, you didn't look like the outdoor type. There's a concert in San Diego Friday night, if you're free."

*What-what-what?* Gloria mouthed.

"Horseback riding or a concert," Mimi repeated to get the message to her audience.

*Concert!* Gloria whispered. *Don't be a hick!*

"If neither appeals to you—" Dusty began.

"Oh, no, that's not it," Mimi said hastily, afraid he'd withdraw both offers. "I hate having to choose, but I guess . . ." She bit her lip. "The concert. Yes, I'm sure of it, the concert would be wonderful."

DUSTY HUNG UP the telephone and sat for a moment, staring at it moodily. Now he'd have to get all duded up again to go to a damned concert, where he'd sit for hours bombarded by music he didn't like.

Son of a—

"Put your foot in it, did you, boy?"

Dusty looked across the glass-topped wicker breakfast table at Morrissy Swain. The wizened old cowman flashed a broad grin that split his face into a mass of leathery wrinkles, his store-bought teeth flashing like ivory.

"Don't rub it in, you old coot," Dusty growled.

"That's what you get for trying to test the little lady," Morrissy declared, not at all put off by Dusty's crack about coots. "You know how these city wimmin are. Horseback ridin'—pshaw! What you thinkin' of, son?"

Well, what the hell had he thought? That his first impression of sleek sophistication was somehow wrong? Not likely, given the circumstances. He'd met her at the country club and she was a country-club-type woman. Offering her a chance to go horseback riding was wishful thinking.

"More coffee, *señores?*"

Both men looked up, to find Maria hovering in the doorway to the glass-louvered dining porch. At Dusty's nod she came forward, carrying a carafe.

She poured the coffee. "What more may I do, *señores?* More quesadillas?"

Dusty glanced at Morrissy, who rubbed his stomach beneath the plaid shirt and shook his head. He'd already eaten four of her grilled tortilla and cheese concoctions.

"We've had plenty," Dusty said. "Go on home, Maria." He'd told her not to come to work at all today, but here she'd been when they returned from their usual early-morning ride. "This is a holiday for you, too—should be, anyway."

"*Sí, señor.*" She took a couple of steps toward the door, her matronly figure stiff. She hesitated, then turned back. Her smooth brown face contorted. "But *señor*—"

"Go on," he said. "I don't need you anymore."

He meant it in the kindest way—that she wasn't obligated to come to work at all today, and she'd already buzzed through the entire house, big though it was.

"*Señor* Dusty—" She burst into rapid, emotional Spanish.

Dusty shifted uncomfortably in the wicker chair. He understood just enough Spanish to get by in a pinch, certainly not enough to follow the details of this impassioned recitation. But he really didn't need to understand the language. He knew she was thanking him for her holiday bonus, although when he'd handed it to her, he'd specifically requested she never mention it again.

Well, hell, she was a good housekeeper. He knew that her wages, added to those of her field-hand husband, barely kept a roof over their heads and the heads of their children. She earned her money and he didn't begrudge it.

But her gratitude embarrassed him. He sat there, stone-faced, even after she'd burst into tears and hurried back inside. A glance at Morrissy's careful expression didn't help matters, either. The old cowboy was examining the handle of his mug as if it were of great consequence.

Dusty sighed and looked at the door through which his housekeeper had vanished. He'd handled her gratitude badly. A little sensitivity wouldn't have been out of line. Disgusted with himself, he slumped back in the chair, stretching out his long, denim-clad legs to ease the kinks left by too many wild rides on too many wild animals.

"I keep thinking one of these days I'm going to figure out how a woman's mind works," he said slowly. "Then I realize I've got a better chance of winning the lottery — and I don't even buy lottery tickets."

Morrissy snickered and stood up. "You can set here and worry over it if you're of a mind, but me, I got work to do."

The little man stomped past the screen door and off the porch. He favored his left leg, which had been broken in three places when he was thrown by a bronc and dragged through a corral fence. He'd been sixty-six when it happened, almost twenty years ago.

Alone, Dusty poured more coffee and drank it with melancholy disinterest. His problems with women weren't exactly new. He supposed they'd started with the first woman he'd ever known....

He'd never understood why his mother had hated Montana and the Circle M, or why she'd spent all those years nagging his father to sell the ranch and move to town. Then one day his father had ridden out on a half-broken Appaloosa stallion and returned the next, dragging in the dirt alongside that horse, one foot still tangled in a stirrup.

It had been a hell of a mess. Dusty's mother had gone crazy, as much from guilt as grief, he'd always suspected. She'd shot that horse; nobody had been able to stop her. And no one had been able to stop her from selling the ranch and every head of stock on it.

Dusty had thought about taking off then, making his own way in the world. He'd been fourteen and already a top hand. He might have done it, too, if old Morrissy Swain hadn't had a good talk with him.

Morrissy had owned the ranch nearest the Circle M, a little old shoestring outfit. He was a gentleman of the old school but didn't mince words. "You fixin' to light out, boy?" he'd demanded.

Dusty could have lied—tried to, anyway. But he'd never told a successful lie in his life and hadn't tried many, beyond the "Sure I've done my homework—don't worry" variety. So he'd looked Morrissy in the eye the way Pa'd taught him and said, "Yes, sir."

Mr. Swain had shaken his head as if deeply disappointed. "You can't do that, boy," he'd said. "You can't let your ma down at a time like this. Your pa'd expect you to do your duty like a man."

Fourteen was too old to cry, but at that moment Dusty sure had wanted to. He'd started to protest, started to say his ma didn't need or want him, that he'd die livin' in a town.

Morrissy had waved him silent. "The time to have your own way is a-comin', but it ain't here yet," the old cowboy had said. "Got to take care of the wimmin, boy."

Dusty had recognized the truth by the way his stomach clenched. Ma'd taught him manners, but his pa'd taught him what it took to be a man. A man did his duty, no matter the cost. A man was honest and brave and fair, and he took care of those weaker than himself. And that especially included women and blood kin.

That was how he'd come to California with his mother and sister Lisa, who was two years his senior. He hadn't understood Lisa, either. She'd loved California, right up to her death at twenty in a freeway pileup.

He hadn't understood his wife, who'd used him and tossed him out like any other consumable. He hadn't understood his daughter—if she was his daughter. Lori must be nineteen now, but he hadn't seen her since her sixteenth birthday.

As always when he thought of Lori, he felt a pang of regret. He didn't know what he could have done differently, but there must have been *something*—anything to avoid her rage. *"I never want to see you again!"* she'd screamed at him as she threw his birthday gift back into his face. He'd simply looked down at the unopened jeweler's box lying on the floor, shrugged and walked away.

Yeah, it was safe to say he didn't understand Lori.

He didn't understand the women who slept with him, when he told them he'd never offer more. And now he realized he didn't even understand his housekeeper.

Ah, but he understood Mimi Carlton.

She was a flirt—one of those sleek, wealthy, bored and beautiful women who took lovers like others took aspirin. How else to explain what had happened at the country club last night?

*She's like her sister*, he thought. Dusty knew Gloria, had for several years, although not intimately. She was what his stepfather, Mr. Chalmers, had called "a good old broad," words anathema today, but descriptive, nevertheless.

Dusty liked Gloria because she made no bones about who she was and what she wanted. At one point that had been him. He'd dissuaded her and she'd taken it with good grace, not resorting to tears or tantrums—taken it like a man, he'd decided at the time. They'd settled into a somewhat testy relationship.

Gloria was wealthy and jaded, but bright and funny as well. He had no reason to believe Mimi wasn't the same. Younger, prettier—hell, beautiful—but equally available. Any woman who'd kiss a stranger the way she'd kissed him . . .

Yeah, there was a woman he understood.

About time.


MIMI WAITED FOR DUSTY to pick her up for the concert, her heart in her throat. She hadn't been on a date since she was a teenager. She'd forgotten how to act; she'd do something stupid, she just knew it. Why was she putting herself through this? Why?

J.D.'s curt voice made her jump. "He's late."

"He isn't late." Although she knew that for a fact, still Mimi couldn't resist glancing at her watch for confirmation.

J.D. advanced into the living room, carrying a stamp album, a magnifying glass and tweezers. Cellophane packets of stamps and a haphazard collection of old stamped envelopes protruded from the album's pages.

The boy was not happy, but she could see him trying to hide it. He looked her over, his lips tightening with disapproval.

She'd dressed carefully for the concert, choosing a simple but flattering black dress that had served her admirably for years. Dusty, fortunately, wouldn't know its history, although J.D. did.

"That was Dad's favorite dress," he said darkly. He stalked over to the coffee table and dumped his stamp paraphernalia onto it. "This guy's not coming, you know. Why don't we go to a movie?"

"He is coming, J.D. We can see a movie tomorrow."

The doorbell rang.

"Nuts." J.D. turned away.

"J.D., wait. I'll introduce you to Dusty and you'll see he's—"

"Forget it, Mom!" He cast a blazing glance over one shoulder. "Just don't stay out too late! You don't know this clown."

He rushed from the room, almost bumping into Gloria on her way in. "I heard the doorbell," she said, looking Mimi over, rubbing her palms together in anticipation. "You look wonderful, girl. He'll be putty in your hands."

*Or a thorn in my side or a lump in my throat or a knot in my stomach*, Mimi thought as panic took hold. To

Gloria, she said, "In my dreams!" and went to open the door.

DUSTY WASN'T ONE to place unreasonable demands on a beautiful woman. He expected her to be able to walk and chew gum at the same time and not a hell of a lot more. Anything else was a bonus.

Therefore Mimi's behavior on the drive to San Diego neither surprised nor disappointed him. When her initial effort at small talk failed, she lapsed into a cool silence. That suited him fine. He'd always figured actions spoke louder than words, anyway.

Glancing over his shoulder as they drove south on Interstate Highway 5, he caught her eye. She'd been watching him, he realized, a slight frown on her beautiful face.

She really was beautiful. If anything, she looked better tonight than she had New Year's Eve. The high neckline of her simple black dress set off the creamy perfection of a longish string of pearls that lay across her breasts, rising and falling as she breathed.

Creamy perfection. His gaze lingered for an instant longer and then returned to the road. He heard her catch her breath on a little gasp and allowed himself the slightest of smiles.

This was going to work out fine. Just fine.

MIMI THOUGHT the concert would never end. Not that she didn't enjoy the music—she'd always liked Brahms and Rachmaninoff. She still did, at least, as much as possible under the circumstances.

The drive to San Diego had been nerve-racking. When her efforts to make scintillating conversation had failed, she'd subsided into an awkward silence.

Once the music began, there was mercifully little need to talk. She still couldn't relax, though. Each time his arm brushed hers she tensed; each time his thigh grazed hers she quivered.

*Cool, Mimi, really, really cool,* she berated herself every time it happened. But she couldn't stop her reaction. The man made her as nervous as a cat. She was sure that as soon as the concert ended, he wouldn't be able to get rid of her fast enough.

He surprised her. "How about a drink?" he suggested as they joined concertgoers streaming toward the multilevel parking structure. "I think I could use one."

"You didn't like the music?" she asked in surprise. He'd been the one who suggested the concert.

Dusty chuckled deep in his chest. "No more and no less than usual. How about you?"

Mimi hesitated. *Oh, what the hell?* She was tired of censoring every word and watching every gesture. Time to tell the truth and let the chips fall where they may. "I guess I wasn't in the mood."

The elevator door banged open and Dusty took her arm and guided her inside. She liked his courtly manners and the old-fashioned courtesies he extended. He performed all the small civilities with a lack of self-consciousness unusual in this age of equality between the sexes.

Three other couples entered the elevator and Dusty stepped behind Mimi to make room. She felt his chest against her back, and his thighs brushed against her buttocks. She swallowed hard and forced herself to stand fast.

He leaned over her shoulder and whispered into her ear, his hands settling lightly on her shoulders. "Which brings us full circle. Are you in the mood . . . for that drink?"

She didn't hesitate. "I'm in the mood," she said.

HE TOOK HER to the Black Hawk Café, an upscale country and western bar and restaurant. "This place's got a little more couth than most of the establishments I frequent," he told her as the waitress led them to a secluded booth.

She gave him a wide-eyed glance. "You don't have to put on airs for my benefit," she said, and he couldn't tell if she meant it or not.

To his surprise, she ordered Mexican beer. When it arrived, she took a hearty swallow and sighed.

"Wonderful," she said.

He could see her relaxing, the sophistication slipping away layer by layer. It made her all the more attractive to him.

"Where'd you develop such an appreciation for beer?" he asked. "You seem more the champagne type."

She made a wry face. "I spent a few of my formative years in Mexico, actually, and beer's great with Mexican food. My husband . . ."

A shadow passed across his face. He could see her pain, but it never occurred to him to offer comfort. He didn't like others to intrude in personal matters and always tried to extend the same courtesies he expected. In this case, however, he found it curiously difficult to maintain his distance.

She looked up after a moment, her brown eyes wide and vulnerable. "I'm a widow," she said. "My husband died just over a year ago. But when we were first married, we lived in Mexico for a while."

"You liked it there?"

She shrugged. "That's the logical place to go, if you want to learn about Mexican food. David wanted to own the best Mexican restaurant in . . . in the world, I guess."

"Did his dream come true?"

"Does anybody's?"

*Meaning yours didn't,* Dusty surmised. *Well, neither did mine, lady.*

The waitress arrived with chips and salsa, and talk turned to safer subjects—California, the weather, Gloria. Mostly Gloria—she seemed the safest topic of conversation while they felt each other out.

When Mimi talked about her sister, all pretension fell away. Listening, Dusty felt himself responding to her natural and unforced charm. Her face had lost that guarded expression and her laughter came easily.

"...and Gloria said, 'Why not? I'm only twenty-one!'" Mimi threw back her head, laughing so hard it brought tears to her eyes. Dusty smiled, although he'd lost the thread of her story.

He hadn't lost the thread of his intent, though. As he watched, she moistened her lips with the tip of her tongue, her laughing gaze meeting his boldly. A tightening in his groin strengthened his resolve.

He couldn't remember the last time he'd looked forward to a romantic encounter with such anticipation.

"THAT WAS FUN," Mimi said as they walked down the front steps of the Black Hawk. She smiled at him, surprised to realize how much more at ease she felt now than when they'd entered. Why that should be so she wasn't quite sure. She'd done all the talking, at first out of nervousness, but then because he'd been such a good listener.

*Could this be the one?* She stumbled on the last step and his hand tightened on her arm. *He has everything I'm looking for—charm, looks . . . money.*

Sex appeal.

"You make it sound as if the evening's over." He guided her toward the Mercedes-Benz parked at the edge of the brightly lighted lot.

"Isn't it?" She cocked her head to one side, a slight smile masking her involuntary response. What was he suggesting? Her breath seemed stuck somewhere in the vicinity of her stomach, and butteflies ran amok.

"I hope not." His warm, slow voice flowed over her. He drew her to a halt beside the passenger door. "We could have a nightcap at my place, maybe even light a fire."

Deliberately, as if giving her time to rebuff him, he slid his hands down her arms, until his long fingers lightly circled her wrists. His open gaze met hers, making his intentions crystal clear.

He wanted to sleep with her.

That realization hit Mimi like an IRS audit. Things were moving too fast and going much too far to suit her. She tried to draw back . . . or maybe she only thought about trying. "Dusty," she began in a warning voice, "I don't think . . ."

"Good. Neither do I."

He lifted her arms and placed her hands upon his shoulders. While she stood there, trying to dredge up a dignified refusal, he leaned down and pressed his lips to her cheek . . . her eyelids . . . and, at last, her mouth.

With a helpless groan, she let her lips part before the practiced thrust of his tongue. A piercing sweetness filled her; her stomach muscles contracted.

There had been no man before David and none since. It had been so long for her—she had forgotten what it could be like between a man and a woman. Or maybe . . . maybe she'd tried to forget what she'd never expected to have again.

It all came blazing back to her, along with a wave of guilt that threatened to swamp her.

This wasn't right. She shouldn't be here in a stranger's arms, feeling purely sexual excitement exploding through her veins. She wasn't some cheap bimbo, she was a wife or had been—she was a mother! With an almost superhuman effort she turned her face away.

Dusty kissed the top of her head. Lightly he stroked her back, coaxing instead of insisting. Although she held herself immobile in his embrace, she felt her breasts tighten in reaction, and her legs began to tremble.

"Don't," she said again, her voice thick with the difficulty of forcing out the single word.

"You sure?"

He massaged the curve of her hip, his strong fingers drawing a resentful gasp from her, despite her best efforts to the contrary.

His soft, low drawl soothed and enticed. "I don't want to stop, Mimi." He forced her chin up so easily that it might not have taken force at all. "We're both adults. The first time we kissed . . ."

She closed her eyes against the sight of him, too powerful even in the shadowy light. "That was . . . that was midnight madness, and this is the first day of the rest of my life."

She put her hands upon his arms and stepped back, her resolve immeasurably strengthened when she was free of his touch. "This is all a horrible misunderstanding. I don't sleep around, so if that's all you're after . . ."

He sucked in a sharp breath and the tension spun out between them to wire tautness. When she felt she couldn't stand anymore, he spoke again.

"I misunderstood." His tone was flat and without emotion.

"But—!" She blinked at him in surprise. Was that all he had to say?

"I was out of line. You have my apology."

She'd at least expected him to argue or offer some sort of explanation. When he didn't she felt obliged to press the matter.

"You weren't out of line . . . exactly. I guess our expectations were different." She frowned. "What *were* your expectations?"

He raised one brow. "I think I made that fairly clear." His frank gaze appraised her, flicking down to her feet and then rising so slowly she felt it almost like a physical touch. "What about you?"

He'd just confirmed her worst fear; he'd had no interest in her as a person, just as a warm body to use and forget. Well, if he could be frank, so could she. She had nothing to lose; they had nowhere to go from here. Not together, anyway.

"I wanted to get to know you a little better and see if . . . well, see if anything clicked between us."

"Something clicked, all right, but apparently not what you expected." He rubbed the long fingers of one hand behind his ear. His eyes narrowed in sudden understanding. "Are we talking the 'M' word here?"

She understood instantly, and her cheeks burned with embarrassment. "So what's wrong with that? Marriage is an honorable institution."

"I tried it once. I didn't like it."

"I tried it once and loved it."

Their glances clashed. He shrugged and turned away.

"I respect honesty," he said, unlocking the passenger door of the car. "No reason we can't end the evening on a civilized note." He glanced back at her, his wide mouth turning up at the corner. "Shame, though. Might have been fun."

"*Might* have been?" Mimi slipped onto the seat without assistance. She felt no qualms about flirting with him, since she'd never have to back her brag with action.

He laughed. He actually laughed as he closed the car door and walked around to climb into the driver's seat. "Would have been fun, then. Right up until you tried to drop your loop over my head."

"I suppose a lot of women have tried that."

"A few." He inserted the key into the ignition. "That's why I put my cards on the table. Anyone who wants more than I can offer is free to walk away, no hard feelings."

"No hard feelings," she repeated. "I suppose there's plenty more where they—where I came from. All cats look black in the dark."

It was a cynical, judgmental thing to say, but she felt justified at the moment—justified until she saw dark color stain his cheeks.

"Is that how it seems to you?" His conscience showed; his integrity had been impugned.

"I'm sor—" *No!* she wouldn't apologize. If it wasn't true, he wouldn't react so strongly, would he? "Never mind," she said. "We both made a mistake. Fortunately we realized it in time, so there's no harm done."

# 3

NO HARM DONE? To Dustin McLain, a man who valued honesty and integrity above all things, a great deal of harm had been done.

After he returned Mimi to her sister's house, he drove home, undressed in the dark and lay in his big bed, thinking about what had happened.

He'd been exposed in his own eyes as a man who used women, not honestly, as he'd believed, but with callous and ruthless disregard.

The most recent had been Carri Gibson. He'd liked Carri, but he'd been careful not to let her get too close. Emotionally close, that is. Their physical closeness had exploded without restraint—until she'd mentioned marriage and set out to make him jealous enough to listen.

How many women had tried some such trick? he asked himself. He'd told each of them, right up front, that he wasn't the marrying kind. Why couldn't they believe him? Inevitably the romance—the affair—ended with tears and recriminations on the woman's part and polite indifference on his.

There were variations on the theme—*I told you how it was*, or *You knew what you were getting into*. Or when the going got particularly rough, *If I were capable of a lasting commitment, you know it'd be to you, but . . .*

Had he reached the point where all cats did indeed look black in the dark, as Mimi had charged? Did it matter which body lay beside his, so long as he had a woman when he needed one?

When his wife had walked out on him almost two decades ago, had she stolen his humanity along with his child? Worse—had she been justified?

Dusty groaned and turned his face to the wall.

BREAKFAST in the Van Husen kitchen the next day was not a pleasant affair. Under direct and relentless interrogation, Mimi finally flared.

"No, I did *not* have a good time and I will *not* be seeing Dustin McLain again," she snapped. "For heaven's sake, Gloria, back off!"

"Well, pardon me. Somebody got up on the wrong side of the bed." Gloria added butter to an already butter-rich croissant. "So what happened?"

"We didn't hit it off, that's all." Mimi stared down at her coffee cup. "I don't think we have much in common."

Gloria gave her sister a shrewd glance. "Did he put any moves on you?"

Mimi looked up quickly. "No. Yes. Sort of."

"Well, which was it?"

"All three, I guess." Mimi sighed in exasperation. She'd spent most of the night trying to figure out exactly what had happened. "He made a very mild pass. When I didn't fall into his arms with a sigh of surrender, he brought me home."

"You're kidding. Just like that?"

"No, not just like that. First he made it clear he was simply looking for a good time. And I made it clear I was looking for something a lot more permanent."

Gloria groaned. "Dumb, girl, really, really dumb. You don't tell them that until they're well and truly hooked, and sometimes not even then."

Mimi lifted her chin. "I don't see why. Once we leveled with each other, we both saw there was no place to go. I wasn't about to jump into his bed as he apparently expected, and he wasn't interested in anything else. I think it saved us a lot of time."

"Then why are you sitting here brooding over it?" Gloria demanded.

"Because . . ." Mimi bit her lip. Shoot, she could trust Gloria. "Because he didn't even try very hard. It was like he didn't consider me worth any particular effort."

"Aha, he hurt your pride," Gloria said wisely.

"Maybe so, but— Never mind. I don't want to talk about this anymore."

For a moment it looked as if Gloria might protest, then she shrugged. "Okay, anything you say. Where's J.D.?"

"Outdoors on that bike you gave him for Christmas." Mimi reached out to squeeze her sister's hand. "You've been wonderful, Gloria, but I've just got to start thinking about the future. J.D. and I can't keep sponging off you indefinitely."

"You're not sponging. I love having the two of you here."

"We love being here, but we've got to call a sponge a sponge." Pressing Gloria's hand one last time, Mimi released it. "Monday I get down to serious job hunting."

"Okay, but you don't have to."

"I have to." She hesitated. "You're sure the country club is completely out of the question?"

Gloria rolled her eyes expressively.

"Then I suppose I'll just have to start applying at all the restaurants in town."

"Yes, I hear McDonald's is hiring."

Mimi laughed. "Come on, there must be something between McDonald's and the country club."

"There's a barbecue joint south of town and a few bars that serve sandwiches. That's all a population of twenty-five thousand requires."

"Then how, may I ask, does Westbrook rate a country club?"

"It doesn't, but northern San Diego County does. The membership comes from miles around for that golf course."

"Oh." Deflated, Mimi leaned her elbows against the breakfast bar and rested her chin on her hands. "In that case, I guess I'll just have to get a newspaper and start going through the Help Wanted ads."

"But what about our plan?"

"What plan?"

"Our plan for you to marry a millionaire."

"I told you, that didn't work. It was dumb, anyway."

"Oh, yeah? Then how come while you were out with Mr. Wrong, you got a call from Martin Montgomery, inviting you to Sunday brunch at the country club?"

"I did?" Somehow masculine attention from any source helped to overcome the feelings of self-doubt resulting from her encounter with Dusty. But Martin Montgomery? "He doesn't ring my chimes, Gloria," she confessed.

"Chimes be damned. The guy's worth a mint and you're going!"

That pretty much settled that.

THE WESTBROOK Country Club put on a lavish champagne brunch, Mimi had to admit. Table after table displayed enormous quantities of mouth-watering delicacies. Chef-hatted servers hovered nearby, ready to cook eggs to order or slice roast beef or pour fresh batter into the waffle irons. Presiding over the whole was an enormous ice sculpture of an avocado tree.

"Everything looks wonderful," Mimi remarked as she and Martin picked up chilled plates at the fruit and salad table. "J.D. would love this."

"J.D.?" Martin helped himself to a scoop of potato salad.

"My son," Mimi said blandly, reaching for a wedge of honeydew melon. Sharing a meal with Martin was one thing, but she wanted him to realize right away all the reasons they wouldn't be sharing much of anything else. She waited for him to express shock.

Which he promptly did. His brown eyes widened and he gaped at her. He really was good-looking, in a blond, *young* way.

"That's great! How old's the little tyke—three, four?"

"Eleven," Mimi said sweetly, selecting several leaves of fresh green spinach.

"No! You must have been a child bride." Martin laughed. "I'm crazy about kids, Mimi. Maybe I could meet the little guy. We could toss around a football or something."

"Or something." His response had surprised her. She was sure the mention of a son would have turned Dusty off almost as fast as any mention of marriage. Why couldn't the nice ones be more exciting? Why couldn't the exciting ones be nicer? Why couldn't a certain cowboy—?

The hair at the nape of her neck prickled a warning. She looked up quickly; sure enough, Dusty stood there.

"Hello, Mimi," he said, his tone neutral. He nodded toward her escort. "Martin."

He looked just as wonderful as Mimi remembered, which was a disappointment, since she'd about half convinced herself that she'd exaggerated his appeal. The truth was that she hadn't exaggerated in the least.

The velvety-soft suede jacket hugged his broad shoulders, and the cowboy boots he wore made him appear even taller. His expression was one of perfect innocence, proclaiming them to be nothing more than acquaintances, meeting unexpectedly in a social situation. But his eyes said something else: *I'm on to you, lady, and don't ever forget it.*

Martin grinned and stuck out one hand, holding his nearly full plate in the other. "Good to see you, Dusty. How are you, Mr. Swain?"

For the first time, Mimi realized Dusty was not alone. Beside him stood a wizened little man, a disgusted expression on the leathery face. He wore cowboy clothes—jeans and a bright plaid shirt and boots—but everything was Sunday best.

Impulsively she offered her hand. "Hi," she said. "We haven't met. I'm Mimi Carlton. I just moved here from Denver."

"Morrissy Swain, little lady." He took her hand into his gnarled one, holding it lightly. He looked surprised by her attention. "Denver's mighty fine country. I'm from Montana myself. I—"

"Mimi, have you seen this lobster bisque?" Martin interrupted. "It looks wonderful."

Morrissy Swain shrugged and released her hand. "Your man's callin'," he announced. "Nice meetin' you."

"He's not my man!" Mimi exclaimed, shocked at the very idea. "I'm a widow." She gave a nervous laugh.

Morrissy nodded and turned away and she added, "Maybe someday we'll have a chance to have a real talk,

Mr. Swain." She was curious about the little man, curious and interested. What was his relationship to Dusty?

"Yes, ma'am." Morrissy nodded and kept walking.

Mimi looked helplessly at Dusty, who'd simply stood by and watched, his face expressionless.

"Old Morrissy's outspoken, but he's right. Montgomery could be your man." Dusty nodded after Martin, who was busy piling oyster crackers atop his bowl of bisque. "He's definitely the marrying kind."

"He's too young," Mimi blurted. Realizing too late what she'd said, her hand flew to her mouth.

But she thought her faux pas was almost worth it when she saw the broad grin split Dusty's face.

"That either means you prefer older men or you're older than you look yourself," he guessed.

"That," she said, putting on a haughty mien, "is none of your business. If you'll excuse me, I've got to get back to . . ." She raised her chin provocatively. "To my man."

"Good luck . . . I guess."

She heard his soft chuckle as she walked away. She should never, ever have been so frank with him about such a personal subject as marriage, but she had a bad habit of speaking first and thinking second. Or third.

She found it wasn't easy to eat with Dusty and Morrissy at a table only a few feet away. Martin didn't seem to notice as he kept up a running dialogue with himself. He'd made his money in real estate and found that a fascinating topic of conversation.

Mimi, who didn't own an inch of land anywhere and had no prospects of getting any, found it somewhat less stimulating. Which was fortunate, because she was receiving enough stimulation already. Every time she looked up, her eyes met the level gaze of Dusty McLain.

MORRISSY POURED his fourth cup of coffee and leaned back with a sigh. "This chuck's almost worth gettin' all duded up for."

Dusty nodded, his attention riveted on Mimi. She looked alternately anxious and bored, depending upon whether she was looking at him or at Martin.

She also looked beautiful, from the top of her strawberry-blond curls to the tips of her black pumps. And every point in between . . . His gaze lingered on the full breasts beneath the silky white fabric of her blouse. Even as he watched, her nipples tightened until he could see their sharp outline beneath the soft cloth.

She shifted uneasily in her chair and crossed her arms casually in front of her, elbows on the table. Only Dusty knew it wasn't casual at all. His glance aroused her. What would his hands do to her . . . his mouth . . . ? Damned shame he'd never have a chance to find out, he thought irritably, realizing she wasn't the only one aroused.

Morrissy frowned. "Why you tormentin' that little gal? Leave 'er be, son."

Dusty pulled his mesmerized gaze away. "You don't understand," he objected. "Only thing tormenting her is knowing I know."

"Quit lookin' so danged smug and tell me what it is you think you know," Morrissy suggested, "'cause I'm seein' a whole new side a' you I don't much cotton to."

"Sorry." Dusty deliberately turned away so he wouldn't be distracted by her. "That woman's got an impulsive streak a mile wide. In a fit of honesty the other night, she told me she was after a husband. I backed off — way off."

Morrissy grunted. "That's what all wimmin 're after, whether they got the backbone to admit it or not. Most of 'em ain't. It was danged decent of her to warn you."

But not very flattering, Dusty thought. Apparently she hadn't felt the same crazy shock of anticipation that had jolted him clear to the soles of his feet and all points in between, when he'd held her in his arms.

*Hell of a good thing,* he told himself. *If she'd felt like I do—like I did—we'd have set this town on fire.*

Now she'd turned her attention in a new direction. He glanced back at her table. She leaned forward, her full mouth curved in a smile, her beautiful brown eyes sparkling with mischief as she spoke to her escort.

Jaws tight, Dusty shifted to stare moodily out the windows, not even seeing the manicured golf course or the rolling, tree-covered hills in the distance. Should he warn Montgomery? Nah—it was every man for himself.

On the other hand, men needed to stick together. Maybe he should just drop a hint.

He rose, throwing his napkin onto the table. Morrissy looked up, a question on his face.

"I'll just be a minute. I'm going to—" A flash of movement caught Dusty's eye and he glanced around sharply to see Montgomery follow Mimi from the dining room.

*Hell.* Dusty sat back down and reached for the carafe of coffee, disgusted with the situation, the woman...and most of all, himself.

MIMI ENROLLED J.D. in school Monday. She didn't know which of them had been more nervous about it, she told Gloria later.

"He's only gone to one school in his life," she said woefully. "Poor kid. How's he going to get along with all these laid-back surfer types?"

"Better than you're getting along with their daddies and big brothers," Gloria said tartly. "Mimi, you never did say what went wrong with your date with Martin yesterday. You sure you won't be going out with him again?"

Mimi shook her head. "It wouldn't be fair. He's a nice guy, we just don't . . . you know, click."

"Okay, then let's move on. I'll arrange for you to meet Maxwell Renfrew. He's older—fiftyish—and a widower. He made his money in—"

"Please!"

At the commanding tone, Gloria stopped short and frowned at her younger sister.

"I appreciate all your help, but my social life will have to take a back seat for a while. I've simply got to find a job."

"No, you don't."

"Yes, I do!"

"Oh, for heaven's sake!" Gloria shot her sister an irritated glance. "I knew you'd be this way. Okay, let's be logical about it. Where else, other than the country club, can you meet guys who are loaded?"

"If this is a test, I fail," Mimi said, feeling grumpy. She never should have told her sister about that stupid birthday wish.

"The Westbrook Farm and Ranch Supply Company, that's where." Gloria looked triumphant. "I've got it all figured out."

She did, too. Westbrook had been primarily settled at the turn of the century. Many of the finest homes were old restored Victorians on what the locals called "ranches."

In this part of the country, a ranch usually meant fruit, not cattle—avocados, citrus and exotic crops such as kiwis and macadamias. Many of the well-heeled West-

brookians were commercial growers, but others just kept
a few groves as a hobby or sideline.

And they kept horses—lots and lots of horses—and
dogs and occasional sheep and cattle.

"So if you work at a feed 'n' seed store, you'll get first
crack at 'em," Gloria concluded. "Hot damn! Am I bril-
liant or what?"

"I don't know," Mimi hedged. "Wouldn't most of them
send their . . . you know, their flunkies to do the dirty
work like picking up feed and seed and stuff?"

Gloria gave her a pitying look. "That's the beauty of
it. All the good ol' boys—which include the guys with the
bucks—drop by regularly for a cup of coffee and a chance
to jaw with Pete Patterson, the owner. It's a man thing.
Makes no sense to us women, who know the proper place
to gossip is over a nice lunch and a few drinks." Gloria
winked broadly.

Mimi admitted the idea had potential, but it was still
Wednesday before she got around to checking out the
place. And then it was only because she'd discovered
how truly limited employment opportunities were in
Westbrook.

Approaching the store in her beat-up old Ford, she was
surprised to find the small, poorly paved parking lot
jammed, mostly with pickup trucks. Apparently it was
as popular as Gloria said.

The store itself was situated against the side of a hill,
with a six-foot-high loading dock across the front. Steps
at each end of the dock led up to the front door.

Pete What's-his-name sure didn't waste money on
decor, Mimi thought as she parked her car. She climbed
out into a beautiful golden day, the kind of day you
dreamed about while stuck in January snowstorms else-

where. Warm, too—nearly seventy degrees, she estimated as she left her sweater in the car.

She'd given considerable thought to her apparel this morning, finally settling for a soft pair of gray suede boots, her favorite jeans and a pink plaid cowboy shirt. She had no reason to believe there'd be a job opening, but she wanted the owner of the Westbrook Farm and Ranch Supply to remember her for future opportunities.

These jeans were definitely the way to assure that, she thought as she worked her way toward the store through a hodgepodge of vehicles parked every which way.

She waited politely while a couple of middle-aged and prosperous-looking rancher types squeezed between a big panel van and a beat-up station wagon. They tipped their Stetson hats as they edged past. *Maybe Gloria has a good idea here*, Mimi decided as she turned toward the narrow passageway—plowing smack into a young woman following the men.

"I'm sorry," Mimi said automatically, reaching out to grasp the girl's arm as she stumbled back. "Are you all right?"

The girl gave Mimi a startled smile. "Sure." She glanced after the two men, her blue eyes anxious. "Excuse me, but my father'll be pi—upset if I keep him waiting."

"Oh, sure." Mimi backed up and let the girl by, then resumed her trek through the parking lot. Her mind had moved ahead to the business at hand.

She needed a job and was running out of options. Maybe she'd better start thinking about trying her luck in Missouri. She could stay with her brother and sister-in-law, but—oh, J.D. would hate that. He was in school and had begun to make friends....

She stopped short, uncertain why. Frowning, she cocked her head to listen. Had she heard some faint sound that didn't belong? For a moment she stood motionless, but heard nothing more.

*A cat. It must be a cat.* She started forward again. And again she heard the sound, almost like a yowl. Almost like—

A baby!

She frowned. Impossible. She spun around, her apprehensive glance roaming over the assembled vehicles. No one was in sight. There couldn't possibly be a baby out here without an accompanying adult. It was a cat. Had to be.

She stepped forward, thinking once more of J.D. He liked his teacher—a man, for once. J.D. needed a man's influence and—

She heard it again and this time she was certain. There was a baby out here someplace, in one of these cars or pickup trucks. She whirled toward the nearest vehicle and peered inside. Nothing on the seat except a rolled-up newspaper and candy-bar wrappers.

Nothing in the next or the next, but Mimi was undeterred. She was absolutely certain that there was a baby out here, perhaps unattended. She didn't dare stop until she made sure everything was all right. If there was a baby in one of these vehicles, she'd find it.

And then she did.

Peering through the cracked window of an old white pickup truck, she looked into the biggest, bluest baby eyes she'd ever encountered. It was hard to know who was more surprised, Mimi or the baby. His lower lip thrust out in a squared-off line. Squeezing his eyes shut, he let out a howl.

Mimi couldn't believe what she was seeing—a baby who couldn't possibly be more than six or seven months old, left alone in a truck in the parking lot of a feed store. She stared at him in dismay. His chubby cheeks quivered with the force of his wails. He opened his eyes, saw her again and burst into fresh cries.

An overpowering rage welled up in Mimi. Anyone who would do such a thing to an innocent child deserved to be horsewhipped. She gave the car door a yank. To her surprise it opened readily—the swine hadn't even locked the door! Anyone could have discovered the baby and spirited him away.

Somebody deserved to do hard time for this, she thought vindictively. She leaned inside the cab of the truck and patted the baby's downy head.

"Don't cry, sweetie. Mimi's going to spring you."

She fumbled with the unfamiliar clasp of the car seat, getting nowhere. Glancing up, she saw the baby regarding her with quizzical interest. Tear tracks glistened on his sweet cheeks and he drew a little hiccupy breath, but the storm had passed.

"There!" She lifted the restraining straps over his head and slid her hands beneath his arms.

He wore a cheap-looking knit shirt, faded and stained but clean; wrinkled corduroy overalls; a zip-front sweatshirt several sizes too large with the sleeves rolled up; and one sock. Mimi leaned down and retrieved the second sock from the floorboard, next to a paper sack she presumed must serve as a diaper bag.

"Okay, sugar lump," she said, chafing his chubby little foot before slipping on the tiny sock. "You and me are about to raise some hell."

She picked him up and he bounced in her arms with delight. Giggles erupted, and she saw two tiny bottom teeth like grains of rice.

Carrying almost twenty pounds of sweet, squirming baby, Mimi marched to the loading dock, up the stairs and inside the Westbrook Farm and Ranch Supply Company. Close to a dozen men loitered around a pot-bellied stove, clutching coffee mugs. Wide doorways opened to the right and the left of the entry, leading to other sections of the store.

She let the door slam behind her and the men looked up, some surprised, some displeased.

"So," she declared in ringing tones. "Which one of you is the pond scum who left this poor innocent baby *trapped* alone out there?"

Jaws dropped; she'd never seen such a display of innocence. But she held the proof of her allegations clasped to her chest.

"Call the authorities," she commanded. "Whoever owns that white Dodge pickup is in a world of trouble."

Her glance traveled over each man, looking for the guilty individual. Expressions ranged from astonishment to outrage, but not one revealed the slightest suggestion of guilt.

"You may as well confess," she warned, shifting the squirming baby onto one hip. "I'm not budging an inch until I find out who's responsible."

"Lady, you are outta your cotton-pickin' mind!" A short, squat man wearing a name tag that said Hi, I'm Pete! charged out from behind a counter along one wall, waving his arms as if he thought he could scare her away. "You take your baby and get along, you hear me?"

"*My* baby!" Mimi glanced down at the baby. Tears puddled in his blue eyes and spilled over; one tiny thumb was firmly entrenched in his puckered mouth. "This is not *my* baby." Her arms tightened around him, nevertheless. "The way you're all acting, I might not turn him over to his rightful owner even if I find him," she added fiercely.

She let the full weight of her indignation fall upon their heads. *"For the last time, who belongs to that pickup truck?"*

"I do." The voice came from the doorway to her right.

Mimi, her attention riveted upon the store owner, stiffened. It couldn't be. It simply couldn't be....

## 4

DUSTY MCLAIN lounged in the doorway, his expression puzzled but wary. He looked pointedly from Mimi to the child and back again. "I didn't know you had a baby," he said with mild surprise.

"I don't!" Mimi hitched the wiggling child around. With a gurgle of pleasure, he reached pudgy hands to grab the front of her plaid shirt, his grip surprisingly strong. She tried to disengage his fingers but he hung on, crowing with delight at this new game.

"You borrow him special for the occasion?"

"This is no joking matter, Dustin McLain! If you think I'm going to let you get away with mistreating this baby, you've got another think coming." She spoke in ringing tones; the fact that she was creating a public spectacle didn't even faze her in her current state of high dudgeon.

Dusty recoiled, his expression conveying shock but no guilt. "Lady, I never laid eyes on that baby," he announced flatly. "I don't even know *you*, to speak of."

"Ha!" She took a step toward him, her jaw outthrust. Her arm tightened around the baby, who uttered a soft "Hmmph!" of protest.

Dusty's eyes narrowed, and a dark flush stained his high cheekbones. "You wouldn't be foolish enough to call me a liar?" he asked in a deadly tone.

Suddenly everything grew very quiet. Mimi didn't care; she had right on her side. She lifted her chin and met his glance boldly. "I could call you worse."

"There *is* nothing worse."

"No? How about child abuser? I found this poor little angel—"

The "poor little angel" interrupted, setting up such a struggle that Mimi had to rearrange her grip on him. In the process of being repositioned, he grabbed a handful of her hair and tried to stuff it into his mouth.

Hanging on to her dignity, the baby and the thread of her thoughts at the same time was not easy, but she managed. "Little *angel*," she repeated, "locked up inside *your* pickup, all alone. The child welfare people could put you away forever if anything had happened to him— for all I know they might, anyway!"

"I don't like to call a lady a liar, but *I did not leave that baby in my truck. I don't even know that baby.*" Dusty looked around the circle of silent men for support, his glance settling upon one in particular. "Hank, you drove in the same time I did. You know I didn't have this kid with me."

Hank, a big bear of a man with a faceful of dark whiskers streaked with gray, rubbed his hairy jaw. His little brown eyes were mischievous. "Wal'," he allowed, "I did see you pull in and get out. I didn't see the little wrangler, here, but he's purty short—could be his head didn't reach the winder."

"Why, you conniving old reprobate—" Dusty looked at the other man in pure disbelief, then rocked back on his heels. "You havin' a good time?" he asked sarcastically. "I don't think the lady is."

The lady wasn't. She was glowering. Dusty didn't know the last time he'd seen anyone so angry. Her brown eyes darkened to chocolate and her soft mouth stretched into a tight, unnatural line.

She held on to that baby as if she expected Dusty to make a grab for him. *When hell freezes over.*

He glanced at the baby and the little critter picked that moment to smile, his two tiny teeth gleaming. Dusty started to smile back but caught himself. He had no intention of getting friendly with some strange baby.

"Look," he said, trying to placate Mimi—this was, after all, nothing but a misunderstanding. "You've probably just got the wrong pickup. I don't own the only white Dodge in the world."

"Is the window on the passenger side cracked?"

"Yes, but—" This didn't make any damned sense and he was losing patience. Most people had the smarts to take his word. "If I drove in here with a baby, don't you think I'd know it?"

Mimi boosted the child up and draped him over her shoulder. "I'm not going to stand here and argue with you. You say he's not yours, so I'll take him off your hands. There are social agencies to deal with abandoned children."

Dusty felt a twinge of guilt that was totally unwarranted. Damn it, he *didn't* know this kid and he wasn't about to take a bum rap. "Just don't mention my name." He tipped his hat in dismissal.

"In your dreams."

"Beg pardon?"

"I'll have to tell them where I found him, and *that*, Mr. McLain, was in *your* pickup. I'm sorry I even came in here. I should have just taken his things and left you to figure out what happened to him. In fact, that's what I'm going to do."

She whirled and strode toward the door. The baby, still draped over her shoulder, flailed away at her with tiny fists.

"Now, hold on a minute." Against his better judgment, Dusty followed her through the door, aware that everybody else was following him. "What things? There's nothing in my truck belonging to that baby."

"Oh, no?" Gravel crunched beneath her feet as she came to a skidding stop at the passenger door of his pickup truck. Balancing the baby with one arm, she threw open the door. "Then what do you call that?" She cast him a triumphant look.

Dusty didn't know what to call it, but it looked like some kind of baby chair. And on the floorboard rested a brown paper bag that hadn't been there when he parked the truck.

Where in the hell had this stuff come from? His first thought was that somebody was going to a lot of trouble to make him look bad. A disbelieving murmur behind him made the hair on the back of his neck prickle.

"That's what I thought," she said contemptuously. She leaned over to pick up the paper bag with one hand. "If you'll help me get the car seat out of here—"

"Just a damned minute! That stuff wasn't there a minute ago."

Dusty grabbed the other side of the paper bag and hung on. Mimi's furious glance brought no results, so she tightened her grip. For a moment they glared at each other over the bulging bag, exerting subtle pressure until the paper ripped, spilling the contents onto the gravel.

"Now see what you've done!" She looked down at the tangle of clothing, diapers and baby bottles. Kneeling, she perched the baby on one jeaned knee, holding him there while she pulled the spilled items toward her, muttering under her breath.

Dusty watched for a moment, then bent down to pick up a grubby envelope that had fluttered off to one side. He handed it to her; she didn't take it.

He stated the obvious. "It was in the bag."

"So?"

"So take it." He dropped it.

She picked up the envelope and struggled to her feet. Coping with the wiggly baby, she tried to rip open the flap at the same time.

Dusty didn't offer to help. It wasn't his letter and it wasn't his kid and he didn't intend to get involved with either. Besides, what could he do? He knew nothing about babies and cared less. Even if he did, he'd be afraid to touch this one. Mimi would probably turn and run, leaving him holding the bag—not to mention the baby.

"Here, lady, gimme the kid."

Hank stepped forward and held out his arms. He beamed at the baby; the baby beamed back.

Mimi gave the bearded man a suspicious look and tightened her grip on the child, who seemed perfectly ready to jump into the arms of this stranger. Five or six other men crowded closer to watch.

"Hey," Hank continued in a cajoling voice, "I'm a grandpa. I know what I'm doin'." He wiggled his fingers playfully. "Come 'ere, you little rug rat."

The baby shrieked with laughter and flung himself forward, almost popping out of Mimi's protective embrace. For a moment she fought to hang on to the little imp.

Dusty's chuckle earned him another glare as she regained the upper hand with the kid. Her response reminded Dusty that this was no laughing matter, and he smoothed out his expression. But hell! This was all some kind of a mistake and once she admitted it, they'd all laugh.

Hank still stood there, arms outstretched hopefully. "Naw, really, I know what I'm doing," he assured her. "We'll go sit on the steps while you and ol' Dusty figure things out."

"Well . . . all right." Mimi relinquished the baby with obvious reluctance. "Be careful, okay? He's a handful."

"You bet," Hank agreed. For a man that big and tough, he sure could put on a silly grin. So could the other men who crowded around to chuck the baby beneath the chin and utter inanities.

Mimi watched for a few seconds as the clump of characters moved in a body toward the steps. Satisfied with Hank's expertise, she turned her attention back to the envelope. Lifting the flap, she peered inside.

"Well, look at this." She fished around with her fingers and pulled out something that flashed golden in the sunshine—a chain bearing a heart-shaped charm.

Dusty felt his blood run cold. Dangling from Mimi's fingers was the necklace he'd given his daughter Lori on her sixteenth birthday. His stomach clenched as if someone had driven a fist into his gut.

*What in the hell was going on here?*

". . . and a letter."

Mimi was still talking; she unfolded a single sheet of paper. He had to pay attention, but his mind seemed permanently stalled.

She began to read: "Daddy—"

She stopped short and stared at Dusty. She looked as if she were about to say something, then seemed to change her mind and slowly continued reading: "I am desperate. This is your grandson Danny."

Dusty's entire body clenched into a knot at those words: *Daddy, I am desperate. This is your grandson Danny.*

Could it be true?

Mimi read more slowly, her tone cautious now and soft. "I need a safe place to leave him for a little while. He's a good baby. He likes—" She swallowed hard.

Watching her, Dusty had the eerie feeling that she was reacting for him, since he felt too frozen with shock to react for himself.

"He likes bananas and applesauce and hates peas," Mimi continued in a rush. "I love him very much. Please, please, Daddy—" she glanced up swiftly as if to lend emphasis to the entreaty "—take good care of my baby. Your *daughter*—underlined—Lori."

"Jesus Christ," Dusty said weakly. He couldn't think what else to say.

"There's a P.S.," Mimi whispered. "I'm sorry, but this is life or death, and I have nowhere else to turn."

Unconsciously Dusty squared his shoulders. He had never felt so helpless or scared in his life, not even facing hell on the hoof in the form of a charging Brahma bull. He stared blankly ahead, wondering what kept him upright.

Hesitantly Mimi touched his arm. "Is it true?" she asked, her voice filled with compassion. "Is that your grandson?"

"I don't know." His voice was a croak; he swallowed hard and tried to catch his breath. The first shock was passing, leaving in its wake an old, familiar anguish. "I have . . . had—whatever—!"

He spun around and walked behind the pickup. He couldn't look at her, at anybody. He didn't want to see her pity, which would be far, far worse than her anger.

He leaned over the side of the truck bed, bracing his hands against the metal, fingers splayed. His stomach heaved and he tightened his muscles, willing himself to struggle past the shock.

The crunch of gravel told him she'd followed, but he continued to stare down at the maze of scratches marring the paint in the truck bed. Seconds turned into minutes. At last a shriek of laughter from the baby—*Danny, the kid's got a name. Danny!*—brought Dusty's head swinging up.

Mimi's low, compassionate voice drifted from behind him. "I'm sorry about the things I said . . . inside. I guess I jumped to conclusions. But when I found that baby all alone . . . I went a little crazy."

"That's okay." Was that his voice?

"Do . . . do you want to talk about it?"

He didn't, but maybe speech would help him get his mind working again. "I haven't seen Lori in almost three years, since her sixteenth birthday," he said. "That's when I gave her the necklace."

He was beginning to pull himself together. The pain receded a little, edged aside by raw panic. Why had Lori done this? What the hell was he supposed to do with a baby?

As if reading his mind, Mimi asked, "What are you going to do?"

He forced himself to straighten, to turn, to face her. "I'll have to give that some thought," he hedged.

She recoiled, shoulders back and slender, jean-clad legs widespread. Her breasts beneath the pink plaid shirt rose and fell with each agitated breath and she fixed him with disbelieving eyes.

Some deep, elemental response stirred in the pit of his stomach. Even in his disturbed state of mind—or perhaps because of it—he felt himself reacting physically to her. Had the shock ripped away all the protective layers he'd built up over the years?

Incongruously, he wanted her more now than the night he'd taken her into his arms and kissed her. At this inappropriate moment he wanted her so badly that his teeth ached with it—his teeth and every other part of his body. He wanted to bury himself in her and forget about cheating wives and ungrateful daughters and—damn, unknown grandchildren!

Which made it all the more fortunate that she'd turned him down the other night, making her position clear as well water. It was the shock, nothing more, that made him vulnerable in a way he'd not experienced since Melinda.

And since Lori, the daughter he'd loved so desperately and lost so completely. He still couldn't believe it....

Mimi's soft lips trembled but she spoke fiercely. "You can't turn that child in to the authorities. He's your own flesh and blood, for heaven's sake! If you did that, your daughter might never get him back."

"She deserted him, didn't she? She may not deserve to get him back." He saw Mimi flinch at his harsh assessment.

"The note says it's life and death!" she said hotly. "Besides, whoever's been taking care of this baby loves him. Anyone can see he's clean and well fed and happy." She bit her lip. "This is none of my business," she continued in a more moderate tone, "but I feel responsible in a way. I am the one who found him."

"Yeah, in the parking lot of a feed store." Dusty was regaining control; his thought processes were beginning to work. "Not exactly the place I'd expect to see you."

"I'm looking for a job." She lifted her small chin even higher. "I wasn't following you, if that's what you think."

He'd like to think that, but he didn't. "Whatever your reason, it's probably a good thing you came along when you did." He cast a dubious glance toward the baby being passed from hand to hand on the steps. "Thanks. I can take it from here."

"But ... !"

He could see her agitation and knew it was for the baby. Grandfather or not, she didn't think he was competent to care for the kid. Her lack of confidence annoyed him, even as he admitted to himself that it was well-founded.

He knew nothing about babies. How could he?

Lori had only been a few months old when Melinda took her and walked out. Dusty had doted on that child. Even after his eyes had finally been opened about the mother, he'd endured the unendurable in his determination to be a part of his baby's life.

Melinda had had other ideas. Her new husband was jealous, she'd said; he didn't like Dusty hanging around. She hadn't asked for child support, just a lump sum "for Lori's education." She knew what he'd won that year rodeoing; she also knew, without caring, what it'd cost him in broken bones and other physical abuse. He had a good chunk of change in the bank and if he'd just write out that check, she might be able to get her new husband to reconsider. . . .

He'd given her the money. It had been every cent he'd had, but he'd figured it was worth it if she'd let him see his child occasionally. Fat chance. Her new husband was a construction worker and they moved frequently, each time "forgetting" to inform Dusty. Just about the time he'd manage to track them down, they'd move again.

He might have kept it up indefinitely if she hadn't got exasperated enough to tell him Lori wasn't even his.

He hadn't known whether to believe her or not. At first he didn't, then he did, and then—hell. But whatever the truth, Melinda's message had been clear. She'd wanted him out of her life so badly she'd been willing to say or do anything to make it happen, even to the point of telling him she'd never loved him in the first place.

She'd married him for two reasons, she'd said. He was good in the sack, and she was pregnant with another man's baby. A man who wouldn't marry her.

He was still good in the sack, but she didn't like life on the Suicide Circuit. Her child had a new "father" now.

"So you might as well hit the road, cowboy," she'd concluded contemptuously. "I tried to be nice, but you can't take a hint."

Dusty hadn't thought about any of this in a long time, and the distress he felt now astonished him. He'd thought that chapter in his life was closed. He'd never expected to hear from Melinda or Lori again. He sure as hell had never expected to be a grandfather—

"Dusty!"

At Mimi's desperate tone, he shook the cobwebs from his mind. Somehow it surprised him that Mimi was so bent out of shape about the baby. If there was one thing he didn't take her for it was maternal.

"I asked, who's going to take care of the baby?"

"I have a housekeeper," he said. That part was easy.

"Live-in? Full-time?"

"No, but—"

"So who'll change Danny's diapers and give him his bottle when this housekeeper's not there? You?" Mimi wanted to stamp her foot in frustration. He didn't seem to realize he was dealing with a real live little human being.

"If I can't handle it, I can always turn the kid over to the authorities," he said in a voice as calm and controlled as if he were discussing the price of avocados. He turned toward the group on the steps and called out, "Hank? You want to bring that kid over here?"

She'd been dismissed. Fear for the baby's well-being threatened to choke her. "Are you sure you know what you're doing?" she cried.

He shrugged and opened the passenger door. Hank arrived and offered the baby. His little face was smeared with something that looked suspiciously like chocolate.

"What on earth have they been feeding this poor helpless child?" Mimi demanded, reaching for him.

At the sound of her voice, Danny turned his cherubic face toward her. He yawned, eyelids drooping over his blue eyes, and gave her a drowsy smile. Before she could react, Dusty took the baby from Hank.

Holding the baby at his side like a sack of grain, Dusty leaned inside the cab of the truck. His muffled voice drifted back. "How the hell do you work this contraption?"

Mimi wrung her hands together to keep from launching an all-out attack on the broad back of the man she considered completely incompetent to carry out the most basic responsibilities of child care. Why, he didn't even know how to work a car seat!

"Lemme give you a hand," Hank offered, casting Mimi a wary glance before shouldering Dusty aside.

While the two men tried to figure out the locking mechanism on the car seat, several others knelt on the gravel and scooped up the baby's belongings, wrapping everything inside a faded receiving blanket.

Mimi watched helplessly. On the one hand this was none of her business; on the other, she couldn't see a defenseless baby spirited away by someone who might end up committing the poor little thing to an *institution.*

Dusty straightened. "There," he said with satisfaction, closing the door.

Through the window, Mimi saw Danny strapped into the car seat. His head drooped; he inserted one small thumb between his rosebud lips and closed his eyes.

Dusty walked around the front of the pickup, Mimi at his heels.

"Well?" she demanded. "What are you going to do?"

He climbed behind the wheel, shut the door and rolled down the window before answering. His eyes, the same blue as the baby's, were stony. "I'm going to do what needs to be done."

"Which is?"

"My business." He inserted the key into the ignition and started the engine. "Thanks again." He looked past her. "You, too, Hank. See you around."

"But—"

He shifted gears; gravel crunched beneath the tires as he backed out. Mimi stood there, heart pounding, while the small knot of men drifted back inside.

But for a moment longer she couldn't move, concern for the baby making her weak.

GLORIA PERCHED at the breakfast bar, a bottle of nail polish before her and the brush poised in her fingers. She watched Mimi pace around the room one more time before exclaiming, "Mimi!"

"What?"

"Will you *please* stop prowling around like that? You're making me so nervous I'm smearing polish all over myself."

"I'm sorry." Mimi sighed. "I can't get that baby out of my mind. I just know Dusty's turned him over to the authorities by now."

"His own grandson? Don't be ridiculous." Gloria dabbed on more polish and held up one hand, examining it with critical eyes. "Does this color work with this dress? Do you think it's too corally?"

"Who cares! Neil won't be looking at your fingers!"

Gloria seemed taken aback but then she smiled. "You're right," she said with satisfaction, adding, "But you don't have to get so snippy about it."

"I'm sorry." Mimi groaned the apology. "I'm worried sick, that's all. Do you think I should call and find out if everything's okay?"

"Absolutely not." Gloria spoke with finality. "I think you should mind your own business and quit wasting time worrying about Dustin McLain. Unless, that is, there's still a chance you two might get together."

"Not even a teeny-tiny little chance."

"In that case, forget him. Nothing's going to happen to that baby. And nothing's going to happen to you, either, unless you start concentrating on the *plan*." Gloria stood up. "Time to run. I'm due at the club in fifteen minutes, and you know how Neil suffers without my scintillating presence."

On her way out, Gloria passed J.D. coming in and gave him an affectionate pat on the head. He ducked aside and glowered after her.

"Why does she always have to touch me?" he asked plaintively.

Mimi said the obvious. "She likes you."

"Can't she find some other way to show it?" Obviously he didn't expect an explanation of his aunt's behavior because he didn't wait for one. Instead he waved a small metal box in the air and announced, "I'm unhinged again."

Mimi grinned. This was his way of telling her he had run out of the small pieces of gummed paper—hinges—used to mount his stamp collection. "Sounds like an emergency," she teased.

"Naw, I wouldn't say that." He plopped his gangly self onto a stool at the breakfast bar and reached for the fruit bowl. Selecting a shiny red apple, he polished it on the front of his blue- and yellow-striped T-shirt. "It can wait until we've got some money coming in."

She started to protest, to assure him that they could still afford a buck or two for such minor luxuries. The earnest expression on his face stopped her. His stamp collection meant a lot to him, but his position as man of the family meant more. He wanted to do his part. She mustn't throw his small sacrifice back into his face.

But oh! how she longed to provide more lavishly for her child. She tried to let none of this color her tone. "Thank you," she said. "That would help."

He shrugged and bit into the apple. "I'm too busy to fool around with stamps, anyway," his words garbled as he chewed.

"John David, don't talk with your mouth full," she admonished, ever the mother. "You know that—" the telephone rang and she reached for it "—makes me crazy." She picked up the receiver.

Silence greeted her. Then she heard what sounded like a gasp, followed by a thunk as if the telephone receiver had been dropped and finally the explosive shriek of a baby.

"Danny!" She shouted into the receiver. "Oh, my gosh, what's going on? Danny! Dustin! What's the matter?"

At her first frenzied shout, J.D. jumped to his feet, his brown eyes flashing. "What—who—?"

*"Morrissy, take this kid!"*

Dusty's roar on the other end of the line made Mimi jump and momentarily yank the phone away from her ear. Then he gasped again and asked, "Mimi, is that you?"

"Of course it's me! What are you doing to that baby?"

She heard him groan. "You mean, what's he doing to us?"

The screaming continued in the background but faded in volume, as if Morrissy had carried the unhappy child to the far side of the room. "Mimi?" Dusty sounded almost normal again, if a bit tentative.

Her first panic had abated. "Is the baby sick?"

"I . . . I don't think so."

"Dusty, please tell me what happened. Very slowly and very calmly, okay?"

There was a slight hesitation. "Maria couldn't stay," he said, as if the full horror of it hadn't yet dissipated.

"And Maria is . . . ?"

"The housekeeper. She . . . when she saw the baby she acted tickled to death, but when I told her I needed her to stay and take care of him for me...she...well, she..."

"What did she do, Dusty? Just say it."

"She sort of busted into tears."

Mimi heard the bewilderment in his voice. "Does your housekeeper have a family of her own?" she asked gently.

"Yeah. Six or seven kids and—oh." He sounded deflated. "I guess she probably had to go take care of them, huh?"

"I wouldn't be at all surprised." Mimi bit her lip to keep from laughing at his domestic ineptitude. "Why did you call? What is it you want from me?"

"Isn't it obvious? I need some help here! Could you... Do you think you could come out here and...you know, tell us what to do?"

She didn't even have to consider. "I expect I could do that," she agreed. *He hadn't turned Danny in to the authorities after all! Hallelujah!* "You'll have to give me directions."

"It's easy." The desperation was returning to his voice, possibly because Danny was turning up the volume. "Avocado Road, turn left on Citrus. It's the big old Victorian at the end."

"Okay, I'll find it. Anything else?"

A hesitation. Then: "Yeah. Could you bring baby food and some diapers? I'll pay you back when you get here."

Mimi held herself together until she was off the line. Then she collapsed with laughter against the breakfast bar. J.D. watched, his expression alive with curiosity.

Finally she straightened and brushed her damp eyes. "Wanna go for a ride?" she asked. "This really should be worth seeing."

# 5

THE QUEEN ANNE VICTORIAN rose in regal splendor at the foot of Citrus Road, a blue, gray and white jewel in a resplendent emerald setting. The first sight of it took Mimi's breath away.

Two stories high, the house looked charmingly eccentric with its steeply pitched gabled roof. Details that would ordinarily command attention—patterned shingling, rounded bays and a single-story, curved, wraparound porch—provided a mere backdrop for a domed tower rising to the right of the entrance, complete with widow's walk.

A larger but more gently rounded extension on the left, accented by curved, stained-glass windows, provided balance for the tower. Ancient oaks and huge sycamores added to the stately elegance.

"Ho-ly cow." Mimi slowed the car to gawk. "Did you ever see anything like that?"

J.D. bounced with excitement on the passenger seat. "Hey, they've got horses!" he exclaimed, his voice filled with awe. "I think there's a barn in back."

In fact there was a number of outbuildings—even a gazebo—but the house held Mimi's attention. Dustin McLain lived here? Alone? She almost groaned with dismay. If ever a house was designed for family living, it was this remnant of a bygone era.

There would be nooks and crannies begging to be explored and towers in which to dream. What a crying shame. She turned up the wide driveway and pulled to a stop. It ought to be against the law, a bachelor living in a house like this.

Only now he wasn't. Now his grandson had moved in.

J.D. flung open his door and jumped out. He looked ready to disappear around the house to check out the equine population, but Mimi called him back.

"You can't just snoop around somebody else's home," she scolded, handing him the plastic bag of disposable diapers they'd picked up on the way out of town. She lifted out the grocery bag containing baby food and formula and other odds and ends. "Behave yourself."

J.D. gave her a disgusted glance but did as he was told, falling in behind her as she climbed the four fan-shaped steps leading to the porch.

More stained glass surrounded the small pane at the top of the entryway. Mimi was admiring the intricate workmanship when the door swung wide. Dusty McLain stood there, a harried expression on his normally unruffled face.

"Thank God! I thought you'd never get here." He reached for her grocery bag and gestured for them to enter.

Mimi stepped inside, onto a richly colored Oriental rug that glowed like a magic carpet. Spellbound by the magnificence of her surroundings, she stared....

Beautifully grained pine paneling created a stately and impressive entryway. An elaborate hall tree and a carved antique chair sat against the far wall, where a hall opened up the way to the back of the house.

To the left, a gleaming wooden staircase rose to the second floor; on the right, a tall grandfather's clock stood like a sentry beside an open door leading to a room that appeared to be either an office or a library. The clock struck the hour—five in the afternoon—and Mimi started at the first mellow chime.

As the final note died away, J.D. stepped forward and stuck out his hand. "Hi," he said with youthful bravado. "I'm J.D. Carlton. I came along to keep my mother company."

"Your mother?" Dusty looked from one to the other, his shock plain. His glance settled upon Mimi. "You didn't tell me you had a son."

"Our friendship didn't last long enough for me to get around to it," she said.

Her sarcasm was lost on him as his big hand enveloped J.D.'s smaller one. "Glad to meet you. I'm Dusty McLain."

A shriek from the bowels of the house brought all three of them swinging around toward the sound.

J.D. recovered first. "Man, you got problems," he said, effectively removing himself from any responsibility. "Personally, I don't like kids. Would you mind if I look around outside while you and Mom handle this?"

Dusty gave the boy a sour look. "Thanks for nothing, kid. I'd prefer to join you, but I don't suppose . . ."

He glanced hopefully at Mimi. When she pursed her lips and gave a single negative shake of the head, he sighed. "Okay," he told J.D., "but don't go inside the corrals. You look like a tenderfoot to me and I don't like amateurs messin' with my horses."

J.D. dropped the bag of diapers and scampered out. Dusty turned to Mimi with the air of a doomed man. "I suppose we should go give old Morrissy some relief."

Picking up the diapers, he led the way down the long hall, finally turning left into the kitchen. Mimi stepped inside the room and stopped short.

It looked like an explosion in a food factory. Dusty and Morrissy must have tried to appease the unhappy baby with everything edible in the entire kitchen. They'd obviously found out the hard way what happened when they turned on the blender without its cover; food sprays of various colors rainbowed across the once pristine white cabinets and marred the beautiful butcher-block countertops.

Mimi choked back laughter as she assessed the situation, but a whimper brought her back to the real business at hand.

Danny sat on a large butcher-block table in the middle of the room, his lower half swathed in terry cloth and his chest bare. He held a teaspoon in his right fist and banged it somewhat dejectedly in the general direction of the dishes before him. More often than not he hit his leg instead of his target.

Perspiration plastered his dark hair to his skull, and tear tracks glistened on his flushed cheeks. He gulped in a breath that was half sob and looked up, his chin trembling. He caught sight of Mimi. Letting out an indignant wail, he threw himself forward.

"Hold on, ya little varmint!"

Morrissy, standing beside the table, lunged for the resolute baby. Mimi gasped and leaped forward, snatching him up just as he reached the edge.

Without regard to her clothing, she pressed the baby to her breast, nestling his head into the curve beneath her chin. "There, there, don't cry, baby doll," she crooned. "Men just don't know anything about babies...." She gave the men in question the benefit of her disdain. "But you're okay now. Mimi's here."

Danny's outraged cries hiccupped to a halt and he raised his head. He gave her a teary smile and stuck his thumb into his mouth.

"What a good boy!" Mimi praised, patting his damp, towel-draped bottom. "Let's get you cleaned up and then we'll figure out what to do with you."

Dusty, standing just inside the doorway, made a choking sound. "I don't believe this," he said in mournful tones. "After all he's put us through, now he shuts up just like that? When *I* picked him up, he upchucked on me."

"What're you complainin' about, boy?" Morrissy stomped toward the back door. "He got me with th' other end!"

DUSTY WANTED TO FOLLOW Morrissy through the door and leave everything up to Mimi, but she wouldn't allow it.

"There's a lot you need to learn about babies, even if you do plan to hire somebody to do the dirty work," she insisted.

So Dusty had to suffer the indignity of her amusement when she went to clean Danny up and discovered his makeshift diaper—they'd used masking tape to hold a terry towel around the baby's middle. Dusty'd been pretty proud of himself when he came up with the idea.

Listening to her laughter when she saw it, he longed to attribute the idea to Morrissy, but an intrinsic sense of honesty wouldn't allow it. Instead he retreated into icy aloofness, silently vowing not to leave himself open to her censure again.

But when she ran a couple of inches of water into the bathtub and proceeded to turn one cross and grubby little ragamuffin into a rosy and sweet-smelling cherub, he felt his ruffled feathers inexplicably smoothed.

She was crazy about this kid. She couldn't fake that; she adored him. She touched him with love and he responded, although frequent yawns betrayed his fatigue.

On her knees beside the tub, Mimi held Danny securely while she glanced over her shoulder at Dusty. Her smile sparkled. "Grab a towel and I'll pull him out of here before he goes to sleep," she instructed.

"What? A—?"

Caught by surprise, Dusty realized he'd been concentrating on the graceful curve of her back and hips as she leaned over the tub. He looked hastily around for a towel and of course found one, hanging on the wall rack. He offered it to her but she shook her head, keeping a firm grip on Danny's pudgy thigh.

"Open it up and I'll hand him to you," she instructed. She turned back to the child. "You ready to get out, Danny-boy? Here we go to Grandpa."

Dusty flinched at the use of that unfamiliar and unwelcome title, but had no time to dwell on it as she lifted Danny into his arms. Instinctively he closed the towel around the child and enveloped him in a bear hug.

Already conditioned to expect tears, Dusty tensed. Instead, Danny heaved a great sigh and let his head drop onto his grandfather's chest, his little fingers clutching.

Something inside Dusty turned over, and his arms tightened spasmodically around the burden that suddenly felt unbearably sweet. Danny squeaked in mild protest, but that was all.

Dusty's gaze met Mimi's, and something tender and eloquent seemed to rush between them. For a bewildered instant he hesitated; then he handed her the baby and walked quickly out of the bathroom.

A HALF HOUR LATER, Dusty sat at the butcher-block table in the kitchen drinking coffee, while Mimi attacked the mess. The back door crashed open and J.D. rushed in, followed more slowly by Morrissy.

"Mom, they've got a ton of horses!" the boy exclaimed. "Mr. Swain says maybe I can learn to ride, if it's okay with Mr. McLain. He says—"

"Dusty. Call me Dusty."

J.D.'s mouth snapped shut and he gave Dusty a dubious look, then turned to his mother. "Can I, Mom?"

"You may not." Mimi put the newly washed lid on the blender and pushed it against the white-tiled back splash. She added for Dusty's benefit, "That's just not the way we do things. It doesn't show the proper respect."

She expected him to acquiesce, perhaps not gracefully. Instead he stood up so abruptly that his wooden chair clattered over and hit the floor.

"Then I'll answer to 'Hey, you,' or 'McLain,' but I won't be called 'Mr.' anything by your boy."

He walked out of the kitchen. Mimi and J.D. stared after him in stunned silence. Only Morrissy seemed unperturbed.

"Got any more a' that java?" he inquired, inclining his head toward Dusty's cup on the butcher block.

"Sure." Mimi poured a mug full and handed it to the little man, who sat down and proceeded to spoon in sugar.

"What'd I do?" J.D. asked at last.

"Not a thing, sonny." Morrissy took a swig of coffee and sighed with satisfaction. "See, Dusty had a step-pa and to the day that man died, he was 'Mr. Chalmers,' never 'Pa' or even 'Harry.' Got his neck bowed about it, is all." He looked around. "So where's the little maverick?"

"Sleeping."

"What's a maverick?" J.D. sat down, looking at the old man with a mixture of fascination and hero worship.

"You don't know what a maverick is?" Morrissy regarded the boy with feigned astonishment. "Why, a maverick's just a little ol' lost calf, is all. You want me to explain what a calf is?"

"I know what a calf—ah, you're teasing."

Mimi left them to entertain each other. She wasn't sure which one enjoyed it most. Quietly she crossed the hall to the maid's room and looked in on Danny.

The baby slept in a makeshift bed—really a pallet on the floor, his space defined by heavy wooden dining-room chairs tipped onto their sides to keep him from rolling out or otherwise escaping.

Tomorrow Dusty would need to buy a crib. The baby's deep breathing was just this side of snoring, and the sound brought a slight smile to her lips.

Any baby was easy to love, but Danny was special. He'd better be—she knew he'd need every ounce of charm if he was going to make inroads into his grandfather's affections. And if he didn't . . .

Turning away, she wondered if Dusty felt sufficiently hassled to turn the problem over to the child welfare people. Her stomach clenched.

In the front hallway she stopped and looked around, uncertain where she'd find him. Some sound to her right caught her attention and she turned toward it.

She supposed the room before her would most properly be called a parlor. Dusty stood in front of the fireplace in dark solitude, his elbows braced on the magnificent cherry mantel and his head drooping. His long, lean figure provided the most arresting feature of an arresting room.

Burgundy and deep forest green combined in both wallpaper and carpet. The medallion-backed settees were upholstered in green velvet, and a marble-topped table displayed what looked to be a family Bible, bound in burgundy leather.

Sheer white lace curtains dressed the tall, narrow windows, topped by burgundy velvet swags. Jewel-bright Tiffany lamps graced small mahogany tables with valanced skirts.

"You want me?"

She jumped at the sound of his voice. "Yes. I mean..." She hesitated, then added with a rush, "J.D. can call you by your first name, if that's what you want."

"I want."

"Okay, I'll make an exception. Consider it done." She half turned. "If you'll come out to the kitchen, I'll show you exactly what to do when Danny wakes up in the morning. You shouldn't have any prob—"

His hands on her shoulders startled her. He swung her around to face him and her lips parted in surprise.

"What do you mean, I shouldn't have any problems?" he demanded. "Where will you be?"

"Home, of course—at Gloria's." She stared at him as understanding crept in. "Wait a minute. You expected me to stay the night?" Offended, she tried to shake off his hands. "No wonder you looked so surprised to see J.D.!"

"I was surprised because I didn't know you had a kid." His fingers tightened fiercely, digging into her shoulders. "Mimi, you've *got* to stay. I need you!"

His strength overwhelmed her. Something about him always made her feel slightly out of control, but this was new and different; now she sensed an equal lack of control in him. He leaned down to stare into her face, his blue eyes beseeching.

She stood perfectly still, realizing the futility of struggle. "Dusty, you're hurting me," she said in a low voice.

"No, I'm not," he shot back. "I'm scaring you, which is not the same thing."

Abruptly he released her and stepped back. Relieved, she lifted her hands to massage her tingling shoulders.

"I'm sorry," he said. "But if you don't stay, I'll just have to . . ." His voice trailed off and he shrugged.

"Have to what, as if I didn't know?" She gave him a withering look. "If I don't stay, neither does Danny—is that the deal? That is the most despicable thing I've ever heard!"

"It would be, if that's what I meant." He gritted his teeth and sucked in a deep breath. "What I'm trying to say is, if you don't stay I'll have to find someone else. And that'd be a real shame, since the kid's already nuts about you."

"Oh." Was he sincere or simply trying to do a number on her? She watched suspiciously as he rocked back on his heels, thumbs hooked in the pockets of his Levi's.

His gaze narrowed. "Didn't I hear you say you were looking for a job?"

That seemed a million years ago, but she nodded.

"You've found one, then."

"You want to hire me as a *nanny* for your grandchild?" she asked incredulously.

"Why not? It's respectable work. This house has plenty of room, so we won't get in each other's way. I'm around a lot, but mostly in the office or outdoors. And I have a housekeeper who comes in three days a week—she'll lend a hand."

Instantly Mimi bristled. "What about J.D.?" she demanded.

"Well, hell," Dusty deadpanned, "let's take him out and drown him."

She tried to maintain her vexation, but her sense of humor won out. "Very funny," she conceded.

At her sheepish grin he continued more gently. "I said there's plenty of room, and that includes room for your son." His expression softened. "By the looks of him, J.D.'s still missing his father."

"Yes." Common sense warned her it would be dangerous to her mental health to get mixed up with this man and his problems, but he was right about J.D.

"Morrissy's great with kids."

Her generous feelings toward him crashed and burned; he wasn't talking about himself. "I'm sorry," she snapped, "but I can't consider it." Back straight, she marched down the hall, intending to collect her son and head for home.

Dusty trailed at her heels. "Room, board, and three hundred bucks a week."

Her heart leaped; it was an outrageous salary for such joyful work, but she remained firm. "For twenty-four hours a day, seven days a week? No, thanks."

"Sorry, I forgot. Money you don't need—it's a husband you're after."

She stopped so abruptly that he stepped on her heels. "*What* did you say?"

"You told me yourself that you want to get married."

"No, I didn't! I told you I *believe* in marriage!"

"Same thing. Look, I can tell you like the little curtain climber, so how about this—I'll hire nighttime baby-sitters anytime you want to go out."

"I've got a better idea." Her eyes glinted dangerously. "When I want to go out, *you'll* do the baby-sitting." At his doubtful expression, she pursed her lips and nodded. "That's what I thought. He's your grandson, but you don't want to get involved. You just want to hire people to do for him."

"I've got a business to run," he protested.

"Ha! A lot of men run businesses and still manage to have a personal life." She took off again toward the kitchen.

"If I agree, will you say yes?"

"No! J.D. would hate the whole idea."

Of that she was sure. J.D. didn't like anything that threatened his position as the only man in her life. He didn't even like the few casual dates she'd had since his father's death. He certainly had no patience with or interest in babies. No, J.D. definitely wouldn't like the idea.

She reached for the kitchen door, but Dusty's arm snaked past her shoulder to hold the door closed.

"Shall we let J.D. decide, then?" he said in a tone so neutral that the hairs on the back of her neck prickled. Or maybe it was the nearness of his lips to her ear. . . .

Before she could think of an answer, he pushed open the kitchen door. Morrissy and J.D., sitting at the butcher-block table exactly as she'd left them, looked up with mild interest.

Dusty stepped up to the table and leaned both palms against it. "Okay, kid," he said, "here's the deal. I want to take you on as a gofer for that old cowboy there. I'll pay you whatever he tells me you're worth and let you ride anything on this place you think you're big enough to handle."

J.D.'s eyes literally bugged. "Oh, gee, gosh, Mr. McLain, do you mean it?"

"Dusty. Call me Dusty."

The boy's eyes darted to his mother. "Ma said—"

"Ma? Since when have you started calling me 'Ma'?" Mimi demanded.

J.D.'s freckled face flushed. "Ah, Mr. Swain calls you my ma and I just sorta picked it up."

Along with the beginnings of a drawl that hadn't been there mere hours ago, Mimi noticed.

J.D. sat up straighter. "My ma—my mother says I can't call you that," he said staunchly to Dusty.

Dusty's smile was angelic. "For me she's agreed to make an exception. And if it's okay with you, she's agreed to take care of the baby, until his mother shows up to claim him." He added, sotto voce, "Assuming she ever does."

"You mean it?" J.D.'s eager eyes searched Dusty's face. He glanced at his mother. "Does he mean it, Mom?"

"Well . . ." she hedged.

Dusty straightened with a hint of impatience. "So what do you say? Have I hired myself a hand?"

Had the sun set in the west?

AFTER J.D. and Morrissy went out to the caretaker's cottage that Morrissy called the bunkhouse, Mimi turned on Dusty. "That was dirty pool."

"Yeah, I know." He didn't look proud of himself. "I was afraid to take a chance. Under normal circumstances, he'd have turned me down cold."

"I wish he had. This won't work."

"It's got to work."

"Because you want it to?"

"No, because both boys will suffer if it doesn't."

That stopped her. She put down the coffeepot she'd been rinsing and frowned.

He met her eyes, his own troubled. "Danny's obvious. We don't know what he's come from or what he's going to. But then there's J.D."

"J.D.!"

He nodded, his fine, lean face pensive. "Boys need the influence of men, Mimi!"

"I'll take care of my son," she flared. "Anything he needs, I'll see he gets."

"I know you'll try."

"You don't know anything about it." She set the coffeepot in the sink. "You sure don't know my son, so how can you be so all-fired certain what he needs?"

"I was a boy once." He gave her a lopsided grin. "I remember how it was when my father died. It changed my mother so much that in a way, I lost her at the same time."

Looking at his face, she could see the pain those memories brought him. "I'm . . . I'm doing the best I can," she faltered.

"I suppose my mother did, too, but I didn't feel that way at the time. Thank God for Morrissy Swain." His blue eyes took on a faraway look, then he shook off the memories and drew a light breath. "This is a good place for a boy. J.D. will be happy here. The minute he isn't, you can walk away and I won't raise a finger to stop you."

*What if he's too happy here?* she wondered. *What if he comes to love this life and this place and this man?* But no, that wouldn't happen. J.D. was excited about the horses, sure, but he was such a self-contained kid that he'd soon get past that initial enthusiasm.

"So will you stay?" Dusty pressed.

Mimi sighed. She shouldn't. She really shouldn't. If J.D.'s heart didn't get broken, hers still might.

But in the final analysis she didn't seem to have much of a choice. "All right," she said reluctantly. "I have a son to support, and jobs aren't easy to find around here. But it's strictly business."

"Strictly business."

He stuck out his hand. After a moment's hesitation she slipped hers into it.

The tremor of excitement that swept up her arm and into her chest had nothing whatsoever to do with business.


MIMI OFFERED DANNY another spoonful of breakfast cereal. He accepted it readily enough, then grinned and let the goopy white stuff ooze out between his lips.

"Are you finally full?" Mimi reached for a paper towel to swab at his sticky face. She'd tied him into a chair with a dish towel across his chest and belly, since no high chair was available. "I was beginning to think you had a hollow leg."

J.D. shoved aside his own cereal bowl and gave the baby a disdainful glance. "I was beginning to think he had a hollow head," he said caustically.

Mimi made a face at her son. He'd been less than enthusiastic about eating cold cereal instead of the hot breakfast she usually fixed for him.

Dusty set down his coffee cup and cuffed the boy on the shoulder. "We've got to stop by your Aunt Gloria's on the way to school. We better move, partner."

"Sure, Dusty." The boy gave the man a quick, eager look. "I just have to say goodbye to Mr. Swain."

Dusty waited until the back door closed before asking in a wary tone, "How'd Gloria take all this?"

Mimi shrugged. "I didn't give her much time to react. She was still out last night when I left the message. My call this morning woke her from a sound sleep. She was pretty groggy." She made a wry face. "It's just delaying the inevitable, though. She'll have a fit."

"I reckon." He drained his cup. "Anything you need from town?"

"Funny you should ask." She dug around in her jeans pocket and pulled out a piece of paper. "Here's a list of a few things you'll need for the baby. I thought you could pick them up while you're out."

"Me?" He recoiled. "Why can't you—?" He broke off, looking embarrassed.

"Right," she agreed. "I'm just the nanny. You're the grandpa."

He gave her a disgruntled look and then scanned the list, murmuring, "Baby bed, high chair, cloth diapers, bottles, clothing sized one year..." He frowned. "Is he that old?"

"No," she said patiently. "He's probably six, seven months, but you never buy babies clothes that fit. They grow too fast, so you get bigger sizes."

"Oh." He raised his brows and shrugged, thrusting the list into his pocket. "You realize I'll probably mess this up."

"No, you won't. I would suggest, though, that since you don't know how long he'll be here, you not buy the deluxe versions of everything."

She pulled Danny's chair closer so she could untie his restraint. He wore a one-piece terry-cloth suit stretched to the maximum to accommodate his solid little body. He looked like a sausage about to burst its casing, she thought with a smile.

J.D. came through the back door, followed by Morrissy. The boy looked anxiously at the old man. "Remember, I get my first riding lesson after school today," he said.

"After you do your chores," Morrissy agreed. "Get along, now."

J.D. walked to where Dusty waited near the hall door. The tall man dropped one hand onto the boy's shoulder with a naturalness that stunned Mimi, and the two left the room.

What was happening here? Boosting Danny onto her lap for his bottle, she stared after them. The sense of jeopardy she felt stunned her, because it was not only for herself but for her son.

She'd forgotten Morrissy was even in the room until he spoke.

"Nice boy," he said. "Needs a man to look up to, though." He looked at Mimi, his eyes bright and friendly. "So does his ma, I reckon."

# 6

MIMI WALKED into Gloria's kitchen shortly after nine that morning, Danny draped over her hip. She found her sister draped over a cup of coffee, newspapers littering the floor at her feet. She looked much the worse for wear.

Mimi didn't have to ask to know her sister had over-indulged the night before and was suffering through a king-size hangover. The truth was, Gloria drank too much. It worried Mimi, but she didn't know what she should—or could—do about it.

She bit her lip. Should she say something now? What? Gloria was an adult, after all. She wasn't hurting anyone but herself.

Gloria did not smile. "You got me so upset when you called that I couldn't get back to sleep. I've been waiting for you for the past hour, trying to read the blasted newspapers and getting more depressed by the minute. Drugs, gang wars—mindless violence. It's true what they say—life's a bitch and then you die."

Her bloodshot eyes finally focused on the baby and she shuddered. "I assume *that* is the cause of all the fuss?"

"He's not a *that*." Mimi put Danny down on the sparkling tiled floor. He looked around, bright-eyed and curious. "Gloria, meet Danny. Dan, this is your Aunt Gloria."

"I am not that infant's aunt," Gloria croaked. "I don't like babies. Take it away. Better yet, give it away."

The censorious tone didn't faze Danny, who flopped onto his hands and knees. He crawled toward Gloria, arms and legs flying as he propelled himself across the floor and through the rumpled pile of newspapers.

He reached her feet and stopped, his attention on her sneakers with their trailing laces. Tentatively he reached out one pudgy hand and picked up a string. A quick look around apparently convinced him he was unobserved; he leaned forward and stuffed the lace into his mouth.

With a yelp, Gloria yanked her foot away, jarring the baby. "He slobbered on me!" she exclaimed. "Do something!"

Danny frowned and turned up his big blue eyes. His lower lip trembled.

Mimi helped herself to a cup of coffee. "Now you've scared him." She had no intention of pampering her sister; Gloria would have to come to terms with Danny on her own. "You're in a great mood this morning. Was it worth it?"

"Don't start," Gloria warned. "I'm old enough—"

She broke off to stare down at Danny. He'd thrown his little arms around her leg and buried his face in her fleece sweatpants. His shoulders heaved with the force of his muffled sobs.

Gloria groaned. "Okay, you little twerp, let's get a few things straight."

She hoisted him onto her lap, scowling fiercely even as she hugged him. Instantly his tears ceased. He gave Mimi a satisfied smile as he nestled into Gloria's embrace.

"Hell's bells," Gloria muttered. "What a little con artist. I'm hard as nails and the kid's already got to me." She gave Mimi a disgusted glance. "Soft touch like you didn't stand a chance."

Mimi sat down at the breakfast bar and reached for a muffin, delighted by the sight of her crusty sister falling prey to Danny's charm. "Dusty's paying me a lot, Gloria—more than I could make anywhere else," she rationalized. "Always assuming I could find anything else."

Gloria turned Danny around on her lap and reached for her muffin. She pinched off a crumb; he opened his mouth like a baby bird and she popped the morsel inside. "But aren't you worried about Dusty making a move on you?"

"Certainly not. He knows I'm not looking for a quickie."

Gloria nodded as if she could accept that as possible. Danny made a grab for the plate holding the muffin and she caught his hands in hers. "Then aren't you worried that if you're around this guy, day after day and night after night, you'll fall for him?"

"I won't let that happen!" Mimi spoke fiercely, because she wondered herself. "I'm not staying for Dusty, I'm staying for Danny."

Was that entirely true? For the space of one quick breath she was back in the parking lot of the feed store, watching Dusty's anguish as he acknowledged the baby's identity. She shook off the unsettling image and plunged ahead. "Besides, it's only temporary. Danny's mother will be back for him soon—I'm sure of it."

Danny, struggling to slide off Gloria's lap, lunged for Mimi. She caught him beneath the arms and lowered him to the floor. "Don't be cross, Gloria." The smile on her lips felt bittersweet. "I just love babies—I can't help it. If I'd had the time and money, I'd have had a half dozen myself."

Gloria regarded her sister for several long moments. "Mimi, you're a fool," she said. "If you come out of this in one piece, you can count yourself lucky."

"Thanks for the vote of confidence."

Gloria shrugged. "I calls 'em like I sees 'em. I just hope you'll at least keep looking."

"For what?"

"For the man of your dreams, dope. This is just a temporary glitch in your plan to marry rich, not the end of it. Dustin McLain's not the only lion in the jungle." She stood up. "Look, I should be on my deathbed instead of standing here arguing with you. If you really insist on doing this, let's get it over with so I can collapse."

By ELEVEN O'CLOCK that morning, the move—such as it was—had been accomplished. Dusty hadn't returned from his shopping trip, and Mimi found herself watching for him as she moved around the big old Victorian house.

While Danny napped, she explored the first floor. In addition to the parlor and kitchen there was a library, a large, formal dining room, the maid's room, where she and Danny had slept last night, a big walk-in pantry and a laundry room.

Upstairs was Dusty's room—an enormous master bedroom and bath connected to a sitting room. But what surprised her were the other two bedrooms—a nursery sharing a second bath with a nanny's room, where J.D. had slept. The nursery was unfurnished, but the pastel wallpaper and antique Jack 'n' Jill prints on the wall gave it away.

Walking slowly back down the stairs, she realized that she was going to end up on the same floor with Dusty—just a few steps down the hall from him, in fact. And most logically, J.D. would be on the first floor, although he'd prefer to move into the bunkhouse with Morrissy.

Too handy. Way too handy. She pursed her lips, wondering if what she'd told Gloria was true—that Dusty wouldn't put any moves on her.

That she wouldn't put any moves on Dusty.

At midday she fixed lunch for Danny, Morrissy and herself. They ate soup and sandwiches on the sunny dining porch, talking like old friends. At the conclusion of the pleasant meal, Mimi carried Danny away to his makeshift bed on the floor in the downstairs bedroom. When she returned, she found Morrissy still at the table. He was leaning back in his chair, a pensive expression on his face.

"Can I get you anything else?" she asked. "More coffee?"

"No, much obliged," the old cowboy replied. "I just wanted to tell you I'm real glad you come. Maybe you can get that bad taste outta the boy's mouth."

"What bad taste?" Startled, Mimi sat down and reached for her glass of iced tea.

"What wuz left by all them other wimmin." Morrissy shook his grizzled head. "The boy was used bad early on and he's been a bronc ever since."

Mimi felt her face flush. "I'm not concerned with his love life," she said stiffly. "This is strictly business."

"You miss my meanin'," Morrissy objected. "I'm talkin' about the wimmin who really counted—his mother and his wife and that girl a' his'n. Whatever he's told you, they was ten times worse. Except the girl—I don't figure it was her fault, her bein' young and all. When she opened her mouth, her ma's words come out. Course, that didn't make 'em any easier to swallow."

"Should we be talking about this?" she asked uneasily.

He stood up, his lined face stern. "I reckon I'm a meddlin' old fool, but you and them two boys is the best thing that ever happened around this old place. I've knowed Dustin McLain ever since he was knee-high to a grasshopper, and it ain't no kinda life he's been livin'. I'm just a-hopin' you don't do him like them others done."

He turned a fierce scowl upon her. "No, sirree, bob, he don't deserve that."

After he'd gone, Mimi sat staring out at the whitewashed fences defining the pastures and fields, the grazing horses and orchards of citrus and avocado trees. But she thought about Dusty....

She was still thinking about him when the school bus dropped J.D. off just before four o'clock. At her insistence he carried in boxes of his books and clothing and stamps from the car before dashing off in search of Morrissy. Frowning, Mimi turned back to the lemon pie she was preparing for the evening meal. Perhaps more hearts were at stake here than simply her own.

A grunt from Danny drew her attention. He sat on the floor surrounded by an assortment of wooden spoons and metal cake pans. As she watched, he lifted a wooden spoon high above his head and brought it crashing down onto a pan, making it skitter across the floor. Laughing, he launched himself after it.

*Make that three hearts at stake,* she amended.

SHE'D JUST PUT a chicken casserole into the oven when she heard J.D. sing out, "Dusty's back!" *About time,* she thought as she turned down the temperature on the reproduction of an antique wood stove.

She looked in on Danny and found him sleeping soundly. Ignoring the fact that J.D.'s things were strewn around the room, she hurried to the front of the house to see what had taken Dusty so long.

Somewhere in the back of her mind she'd expected him to "buy out the stores," but that hackneyed phrase took on new meaning when she walked through the front door.

Dusty's pickup truck was piled high with crates and cartons and boxes and heaven only knew what else. Mimi's mouth dropped open.

Dusty vaulted lightly onto the bed of the truck. "Wanna give me a hand here, partner?" he called to J.D.

"Sure." J.D., face flushed with pleasure, moved around to the open tailgate. "What d'ya want me to do?"

"Maybe you can find some use for this."

Dusty bent down and lifted a small saddle from between the bulky cartons. He tossed it onto the tailgate as if it were of little consequence.

J.D.'s eyes widened until they dominated his thin face. He reached for the saddle with covetous hands.

"But . . . but this is a *saddle*. That kid's too little to use it!" he protested.

Watching, Mimi heard what he didn't add. *But I'm not! Why do some people have all the luck?* Her heart twisted in her breast.

"The kid I've got in mind is just the right size to use it," Dusty said. "Everybody who works for me has to be well mounted. If you think it'll do . . ."

"*If it'll do!*" J.D. dragged the saddle to the edge of the tailgate, touching the tooled leather as if it were pure gold. "Oh, gosh, Dusty—gee, I—" He stopped and swallowed hard.

J.D. and Dusty smiled at each other. Watching, Mimi blinked hard and pressed her lips together to keep them from trembling.

Dusty looked at her and his grin broadened. "Sorry it took me so long, but I went all the way to San Diego," he explained. "Hope I got the right stuff."

"You've got enough here for two babies—maybe three." She hoped her sharp tone concealed how moved she'd been by his gift. "Don't you think you went a trifle overboard?"

"Just trying to be efficient. I don't want you sending me back to the store tomorrow."

"What's left to buy? With all this stuff you could open your own store."

That opinion was verified when all the items were unloaded. It looked as if he'd bought one of everything in the store, and in each case, the most expensive.

The ornate, Victorian-style crib matched the chest of drawers and dressing table. A high-tech stroller boasted a suspension system many automobiles could envy, the high chair converted into a youth chair, and there were various other seats and swings and bathtubs and toys and clothes; the list seemed endless.

Mimi knelt beside Dusty while he spread out an instruction sheet. She shook her head. "You must have spent a fortune," she complained. "Talk about overkill."

He shrugged. "It's only money."

"Then spend it on something that'll really benefit Danny," she flared, angry because he could say that and she couldn't and never had been able to. "Open a college fund for him."

Dusty eyed her warily. "Okay. I'll take care of that tomorrow."

Mimi stifled a groan. Why couldn't J.D. have someone waiting in the wings to underwrite his education? Why couldn't J.D. have soneone—? She pulled such self-pitying thoughts up short. It was, after all, her obligation to locate such a person, and she'd better get to it.

"Will that satisfy you?"

"Huh?" She hadn't been listening, she'd been fuming.

"I've never been a grandfather before—hell, I was only a father for about fifteen minutes. Anything else I'm overlooking?"

"Nothing that money can buy." She hated the sarcasm in her voice. "If you really want to do what's best for him, read stories to him, play games with him, take an Infant CPR class—love him."

Dusty dropped the screwdriver and swiveled toward her. His long-lashed blue eyes were on a level with hers and he no longer smiled. For a long moment their gazes locked.

Mimi was first to drop her eyes. She didn't really know why she'd come down so hard on him. He'd shown some very good intentions and instincts, yet here she was, berating him.

He stood up. "Sometimes you have to settle for what you can get."

"God only knows that's true." She also rose, standing well apart from him. "Honestly, though, you didn't need to spend so much on all this stuff. Danny's only here temporarily."

"Is he?" His voice was too casual as he began to tear open the carton containing the high chair.

"You've learned something!" In her excitement, Mimi touched his elbow. "Have you found Lori?"

"No." His composed expression didn't change. "But I've got people looking for her, and if she turns out to be anything like her mother—"

An agonized shriek sliced through the air. As one they swung around—just in time to see a tiny tornado barreling down the hall toward them.

"Danny?" Mimi looked at Dusty for verification.

It was Danny, all right, galloping along as fast as his stubby arms and legs would carry him. He looked as if he'd been caught in an explosion in a post office. He was covered with stamps—stamps on his arms and legs, sticking on his face and undershirt, even in his mouth. He clutched a cellophane sheet of stamps in one hand, his fist clunking against the hardwood floor as he accelerated.

Grinning—laughing, he came on. The shriek of anguish had not been his, but J.D.'s.

J.D. appeared in the hallway behind the escaping junior felon, all but breathing fire. He carried the pitiful remains of a once-flourishing stamp collection—mangled sheets and empty stamp containers, crumpled stamps drifting down around his feet, scrapbooks torn asunder.

"I'll kill that kid!" J.D. roared, starting forward. "He's destroyed my stamp collection—my life's work!"

Danny reached Mimi and threw out his arms, blissfully unaware of the potential threat to his tiny person. She snatched him up and brushed ineffectually at the clinging stamps.

"Now, J.D., try to calm down," she sought to soothe the infuriated boy descending upon her. "It's not Danny's fault," she added, tightening her arms around the wiggly little body. "He's just a baby! You shouldn't have left your stamps where he could get at them."

J.D. skidded to a stop, staring at her as if she'd just stabbed him. "*You*, my own mother, are taking *his* side?" he accused.

His words cut her to the quick. "No, honey, of course not," she hurried to protest. "But—"

"You are! That brat's to blame, not me! Why aren't you mad at him?"

"J.D., calm down...."

"I'll tell you why—because you like him more than you like me! Fine." J.D. took a step back and threw stamps and scrapbooks onto the floor. His thin body trembled and he looked close to tears. "Let the obnoxious little brat have everything. What do I care? Stamps are for kids, anyway."

He whirled and ran down the hall.

"J.D.!" She was torn between compassion for his pain and indignation over his rebellious behavior. "You come right back here, young man! You can't talk to your mother that way!"

The kitchen door slammed. "Oh, for heaven's sake," she exclaimed, turning toward Dusty for support.

He'd remained in the background during the entire episode. She thrust the baby at him. "Here, take Danny. I've got to have a talk with my son."

Dusty shook his head and kept his arms by his sides. "Leave the kid alone," he said in a flat voice. "He needs time to cool off."

"Says who? Where did you learn so much about raising boys?"

He cocked his head to one side, his expression perfectly contained. "You keep forgetting I was one once."

His quiet reminder pierced her self-absorption and warmed her cheeks. "Look," she said more reasonably,

"I can't let him get away with that. He was rude and in-sensitive."

"No. He was rude, but you were insensitive. He had every right to be pissed. He didn't have the right to spill blood, but I don't think it would have come to that."

Dusty plucked a stamp from Danny's hair. The baby gurgled and batted at the large hands.

"Maybe not," Mimi admitted, "but I can't let him think that's acceptable behavior. I've got to do something."

Dusty raised his brows. "Like what? J.D. sure as hell's gonna hate that baby's guts from here on out, unless something happens to change his mind. I just don't think his mama giving him orders will do the trick."

"I wasn't going to order him to do anything," she pro-tested, "except possibly mind his manners."

"Let Morrissy do it." Dusty retrieved the screwdriver he'd dropped.

"Morrissy?"

"Unless I miss my guess, the kid's in the bunkhouse right now, pouring his heart out."

"I don't know...." She took an indecisive step.

"Don't."

Dusty put his hand on her shoulder. His touch burned through her cotton shirt, jolting her all the way to the soles of her feet.

Desire flashed through her bloodstream. She stared at him, stricken, while her arms tightened violently around the baby. Danny uttered a soft grunt and twisted around to stare at her.

She'd hardly even remembered he was there.

Dusty had, though; he'd remembered the baby and the boy, and he still remembered what it was like to lose—or think you'd lost—a mother's love. He looked into

Mimi's lovely, troubled face and dug his fingers into the delicate curve of her shoulder.

*Don't blow this, McLain,* he warned himself. *You need this woman.* To care for the baby, he added hastily; nothing more. Strictly business.

So why did he feel this yearning when he looked into her upturned face? His glance touched lips tender and trembling, as if in response to a kiss. He let his gaze slide lower, past the throbbing pulse at the base of her graceful throat, on down to the V of her blouse.

She held Danny clasped against her left breast, her blouse pulled askew, exposing one edge of her bra and cleavage he'd never seen before. The satin globes looked firm and resilient, as if they would swell to fit the shape of a man's hand . . . a man's mouth.

She gasped and he realized his hard grip was hurting her. He dropped his arm and stepped back, his gut clenching.

"I know how J.D. feels because I've been there," he said. "It's jealousy, pure and simple, but that doesn't make it any easier to deal with when you're young and hurting."

Or not so young and hurting, he amended silently.

"But . . ." She frowned and he bent over to put Danny on the floor. With fluttery hands she brushed at the stamps still clinging to him, then straightened. "J.D. knows we're only here temporarily. He certainly knows I love him. This baby is no threat."

"I won't argue any of that." Dusty shifted restlessly, knowing he was about to say too much, reveal too much. "Look, I was four or five years older than J.D. when my father died, but I remember how lost I felt. Not long after that I lost my sister in a freeway accident, and then my mother remarried and I lost her, too."

For a moment he stared into space. "Mr. Chalmers." It came out a harsh grunt. "She married Harry Chalmers. I hated that son of a— To the day he died, he was Mr. Chalmers."

"His choice or yours?"

"His." Dusty had never thought he'd had a choice, but now it dawned on him that eventually he had had. Bone-deep honesty made him add, "At first. Then I grew up and didn't give a flying—"

Damn, he hadn't realized how angry he still was. The man was long dead and still the anger remained.

"I'm sorry," she said.

She touched his arm and he went stiff and still, his gaze on her slender fingers where they curved lightly over his darker flesh. He wanted to cover her hand with his and pull her down onto the Oriental carpet and... *He needed a woman!*

She swallowed hard. "You're scary when you get that fierce expression on your face," she whispered. "You're probably right about J.D. He...he's a good boy. He misses his father so much...."

Dusty nodded; he didn't trust himself to speak. Damn, he didn't want to hear about her problems or feel this powerful empathy toward her son.

Her eyes were wide and vulnerable. "So you're suggesting I do nothing?"

*I'm suggesting we both do nothing, because if we ever did...* But he said, "I'm suggesting you wait for the boy to come to you—and he will. Morrissy will send him."

"How do you know that?"

"Because the old man's spent a lifetime counseling boys on what it takes to be a man."

"You?"

"Among others."

"Okay." Awkwardly she uncoiled her fingers and removed her hand from his arm.

Danny had shoved back a corner of the rug and was working hard to crawl under it. Mimi retrieved him. He'd left a trail of stamps all the way down the hall and across the carpet, and many still stuck to him.

"I'll replace J.D.'s stamp collection," Dusty said, "but the stamps were only an excuse."

"Take it up with J.D. I'm going to finish supper. Why don't you go tell Morrissy and J.D. we'll eat in ten minutes?"

He watched her walk away, her back straight and shoulders rigid. Tense. She looked as tense as he felt.

MIMI PULLED THE CASSEROLE out of the oven just as J.D. and Morrissy shuffled into the kitchen. Danny was already strapped into his new high chair, a double-handled cup of milk on the tray. Dusty was struggling to tie a bib around the baby's neck.

J.D. stood uneasily, head hanging, while Morrissy pulled out a chair and sat down.

Mimi placed the dish upon the table and paused before her son. "Yes?" she inquired, careful to keep her voice nonthreatening.

J.D. swallowed hard and sucked in a deep breath. "I'm sorry," he burst out.

He gave Morrissy a quick glance and the old man nodded almost imperceptibly. "A man don't—a man doesn't take his—his frustrations out on women or children. You're my ma—my mother and I love you and I'm sorry I . . . sorry I . . ."

He was about to lose it, and if he did, so would she. "J.D.," she began in a trembling voice, "honey—"

A crash defused the moment. Danny, one hand clutching a handle of his cup, swung it high over his head and brought it smashing down on the tray before him. The resulting racket startled, then delighted him.

J.D. scowled at the baby. "But I still don't like *him*." Giving Morrissy a quick, defiant look, the boy sat down and dropped his napkin onto his lap.

DESPITE the rocky beginning, it didn't take long to settle into a routine that pleased them all. J.D. seemed especially happy, although he pointedly ignored Danny. The boy spent most of his spare time outside with Morrissy, who was teaching him to ride and rope.

Dusty was always underfoot, it seemed to Mimi, and she had mixed feelings about that. Although he had offices in San Diego, he rarely used them. Most of his business affairs were conducted from the combination office-library across from the parlor. He'd installed a fax machine, computer with modem and special telephone line with its own answering machine.

His assets, Mimi soon realized, were many and varied. He owned acres and acres of land, some in citrus groves and other farming operations, some already developed into planned housing communities and shopping centers. He also held a number of business franchises.

The man had more money than he'd ever spend, but it seemed to mean very little to him, beyond the freedom to do what he wanted to do when he wanted to do it. That included joining Morrissy and J.D. for frequent horseback rides and, Mimi supposed, joining one beautiful woman or another in the sack when the spirit moved him.

Disgusting.

Then there was Maria, the housekeeper, quite unperturbed by the addition of three members to the formerly quiet household. She was especially delighted to discover Mimi spoke Spanish.

"Señor Dusty thinks he does but . . . ehh!" She rolled her eyes and gestured with one hand. "Half the time I don't know what he's trying to tell me. The other half, he doesn't know what I'm trying to tell him!"

And she went about her work, laughing aloud.

As Mimi had anticipated, she and Danny moved into the two upstairs bedrooms. Although it was the only sensible thing to do, she had a difficult time accepting it.

It was Dusty's fault. Dusty made her so aware of herself as a woman that the first night in her new bed, she spent hours lying in the dark, thinking about him asleep only a few thin walls away.

*Call it by its rightful name*, she tortured herself. Desire . . . that awful, empty ache that sent her prowling to the window in the dead of the night, that made her groan with frustration when her cotton nightgown rubbed like sandpaper across the swollen tips of her breasts.

While only a few feet away, the instigator of all this consternation slept like a baby. Heaven help her, she had to do something.

A WEEK AFTER SHE MOVED IN, Dusty invited her to go horseback riding. They were sitting at the breakfast table, Dusty drinking coffee and reading the morning newspaper, while she shoveled applesauce into Danny's mouth.

"No, thanks," she said.

He just looked at her, shrugged as if he didn't much care, and reached for his coffee cup. In fact he was furious at her rejection. Maybe his mood was so bad because he hadn't had a decent night's sleep since her arrival.

She scooped up another spoonful of baby goop. "I'd like you to baby-sit tonight."

"What for?" Not that he had anything better to do; he just didn't want the responsibility. It was easy enough to provide economically for the baby, but quite another to be expected to *handle* him. That explained his reluctance; he sure as hell wasn't jealous of her time.

"I have plans," Mimi said.

The back door opened and Morrissy and J.D. entered. Dusty ignored them. "What plans?" he snarled.

Mimi glared at him. Morrissy looked at Dusty with mouth agape, reminding him that he was acting completely out of character.

She pressed her soft lips together in an exasperated line. "If you must know, I have a date."

Two men and one boy stared at her as if she'd confessed to joining a motorcycle gang.

One baby giggled and tossed a biscuit into the air. It landed in Dusty's coffee cup with a leaden plop, which more or less symbolized how his life was going these days.

# 7

MAXWELL RENFREW didn't deserve what he walked into that night. *Nobody* deserved it, Mimi thought, watching her date's smile waver before the unfriendly scrutiny of two other men, a boy and a baby.

The baby seemed to have sensed the brooding displeasure of his elders. His chubby cheeks quivered and he let out a warning yowl.

J.D. cast Danny a look meant to quell; when it didn't the boy's lip curled disdainfully. "I'm outta here," he said and put actions to his words.

Morrissy's dubious glance took in the entire room before settling upon the wailing baby. "Gotta see a man about a horse," he declared, and beat his own hasty retreat.

Mimi turned to Max, who seemed to be overcoming his initial shock. "Do you know Dusty McLain, my boss?" she stressed the last word.

"Sure do. How's it going, Dusty?" Max spoke cheerfully, as if he weren't competing with Danny's noisy outrage. He offered his hand.

"Can't complain." Dusty looked down at the shorter man. The two shook hands. "You?"

Max shrugged and smiled. A handsome, gray-haired man of perhaps fifty-five, he had an appealing air of self-confidence without a trace of arrogance. Mimi had liked him the minute she saw him—which had been approximately three minutes ago. She had to give that little old matchmaker, Gloria, credit. As blind dates went, this one held promise.

Max turned to Mimi, as unflappable as if he frequently found himself trying to outshout a baby. "Ready to go?"

She nodded and turned toward the door, but Dusty's incredulous voice stopped her.

"You're not just going to walk out on us?"

"You know what to do," she reminded him. "I told you exactly, minute by minute."

"But he's crying!"

That little touch of desperation nearly undid her. The baby was making him vulnerable in a way that conflicted sharply with his usually unflappable reserve. He was no longer the self-assured, self-sufficient loner; he was a man of flesh and blood, a man who could be hurt like other men.

By a baby, she reminded herself. Never again by a woman.

Hardening her heart, she shrugged. "You know what to do," she repeated. "I'll see you tomorrow." She walked away with Danny's cries echoing in her ears.

DUSTY COULDN'T BELIEVE IT. Until she was actually gone, he couldn't believe she'd abandon them.

Disconsolate, he knelt and looked into the eyes of the baby who might or might not be his grandson. Danny gulped back a sob and tried a tentative smile.

It was a mystery to Dusty how a baby could go from grief to joy in the blink of an eye. The little fakers were completely lacking in consistency, so far as he could tell.

He frowned. "Okay, kid," he said, "what's your problem? She's coming back, you know." He held out his hand, forefinger extended for Danny to grab—which he did.

*Yeah,* Dusty thought, *she's coming back . . . this time. But what if she hits it off with ol' Max? What if she marries him, for chrissake? That's what she's after—she made no bones about it.*

So what? Even if Max turned out to be the man of her dreams, nothing was going to happen overnight. Dusty needed time, but not a lot of time; he had no intention of letting this situation with the baby drag on indefinitely. He had attorneys on the case, private investigators. He'd hear something soon.

He'd even laid out his own deadline. If Lori didn't surface by the first week of February, he'd have to consider taking . . . steps. Or by the fifteenth, but that was it.

Period.

He only needed Mimi for a lousy three or four weeks. Of course, he'd miss J.D. when they left, but . . . He stood up abruptly. He'd be damned if he'd let her get under his skin this way.

"Morrissy, J.D.," he called into the silent house. "You two shirkers get back in here. If you think I'm gonna play nursemaid all by my lonesome, you got another think comin'!"

J.D. popped around the door so quickly that Dusty knew the kid'd been lurking outside.

Morrissy followed, shaking his head and clucking like an old lady. "What you caterwauling about?" he groused.

Dusty glanced at his watch. "It's after seven. I think it's time to put Danny down."

"Let me do it," J.D. said quickly. He stepped forward and pointed a finger at the baby. "Danny, you're short!"

There was a moment's stunned silence before J.D. and Dusty exploded with laughter. Morrissy looked baffled.

"Don't you get it?" J.D. gasped. "It's a *put-down*." And he succumbed to fresh gales of laughter.

It was too much for Morrissy. He simply turned around and walked out, shaking his head and muttering under his breath.

Dusty picked up the baby and draped one arm around J.D.'s shoulder. He felt a hell of a lot better after that good laugh. "Okay, kid, you got me on that one. How 'bout we drown our sorrows in some of that ice cream your mom's been hiding in the back of the freezer?"

"Great! And afterward I can put old Danny down some more—Danny, you couldn't carry a tune in a bucket! Danny, you can't walk and chew gum—shoot, you can't walk *or* chew gum! Danny, you're—"

They moved down the hallway together, the man and the two boys who were playing hell with his peace of mind.

MIMI TWISTED AROUND in Max's Cadillac to finish her story. "And little Gloria took off around the house with Mother hot on her heels waving that switch—left me standing there crying, because I'd already taken my licking and I knew Gloria was going to get off scot-free again...."

Max howled with laughter. When he could catch his breath, he grinned at her. "I haven't had such a good time in years." He dashed one hand at his cheeks as if wiping away tears. "You and Gloria must have been a real handful when you were kids."

Mimi arched one brow. "There are those who say we still are."

"Well, now, that's the truth." He gave her an admiring look and turned into the driveway before the towering bulk of Dusty's Victorian. All the lights had been left on; the driveway and the front of the house were brightly lit, as was the interior. "I could sit and listen to you all night," Max added.

"You have. It's after eleven. I got carried away."

Max switched off the engine and headlights. Turning toward her on the seat, he smiled. "I've had a great time. This is one blind date that's going to work out fine."

Dutifully she returned his smile.

"*Real* fine."

Her smile wavered. "Uh, Max . . ."

"Am I wrong? Gloria said there wasn't anything going on between you and Dusty."

"Oh, there isn't," she said quickly. "He was in a bind with the baby—it's strictly business. Only . . ."

She bit her lip, trying to decide how much to say. Max was a nice guy, a really nice guy. She liked him. She might even grow to like him a lot. But she was never going to love him. Not while Dusty McLain was alive, anyway.

He caught her hands in his and leaned forward. "Say what's on your mind, honey. You don't have to tippy-toe around with me."

"I'll remember that." He was going to kiss her if she didn't do something. She slipped her hands from his light grip and shifted toward the door.

"Hey, what'd I do?"

At his plaintive question she turned impulsively. "I don't want to give you the wrong idea," she said. "I haven't dated much since my husband died. I don't know the rules anymore, so I don't know what you . . . what you expect from me. At the risk of sounding ridiculous, I feel obliged to tell you that I'm looking for a husband, not a paramour."

"A para—!" He flinched. "What in the world makes you think—?"

"Nothing!" Mortification warmed her cheeks. "If I've jumped to the wrong conclusion, I apologize. I just thought you should know." She flung open the car door and jumped out.

"Wait a minute!"

She did, uncomfortably. When he was beside her, embarrassment made her look away.

"Mimi," he said in a voice filled with wonder, "you are the most . . ."

She looked at him sharply, waiting for some offensive epithet to fall from his lips: presumptuous, conceited, ridiculous . . .

". . . the most *honest* woman I think I've ever had the pleasure of knowing."

"You mean you're not offended?" Together they moved toward the front door, and she added sheepishly, "It seemed only fair to warn you."

He draped a friendly arm around her shoulders. "Warn me! I don't take that as a warning, honey. It's more like a tempting possibility. My wife died ten years ago, and my daughter's grown and gone. There's not a reason in the world I shouldn't indulge myself—in marriage or anything else that appeals to me."

"Oh." That wasn't the response she'd expected. "In that case . . ."

She halted on the steps, one level above him. Clasping his head between her hands, she leaned forward and planted a quick, hard kiss upon his lips. Before he could respond, she stepped back and gave him a mischievous smile.

"I may be old-fashioned, but I'm not a complete prude," she informed him, using her thumb to wipe lipstick from his mouth. "Thanks for a lovely evening."

He was still staring after her with a dazed expression when she closed the front door behind her. Smiling, she turned away and walked right into Dusty McLain's arms.

"Have a good time?" he asked coldly. He knew what kind of time she'd had; he'd been watching through the stained-glass windowpanes.

"You scared me!"

She lifted one hand to his chest and pushed him away, but not before he'd felt the soft heat of her breasts and the suggestive pressure of her thighs. She leaned against the door, her hands clasped at the small of her back. He found her stance somehow challenging . . . and suggestive.

She let her glance flick over him. "Don't tell me you waited up for me."

"Okay, I won't tell you." Although, of course, he had. Some perversity in his nature made him add, "You didn't answer my question."

"What question?"

"Did you have a good time?" It sounded more like an accusation than a request for information.

"Not that it's any of your business, but yes, I had a good time. Max is a very nice man."

Dusty grunted; whether in agreement or disagreement he couldn't have said.

"He is," she insisted.

"Did I say otherwise?"

"No, but—forget it. It's late—time for bed."

"Past time."

They stared at each other, as if neither understood what had just been said.

"I didn't mean . . ." she began breathlessly.

"I did." He shoved one hand through his hair to keep from grabbing her. "It's been a hell of an evening around here—Morrissy bitching, J.D. sulking, Danny whining." Okay, so he was exaggerating; he had a point to make. And he made it. "I hope you're not planning to run out on your responsibilities on a regular basis."

Anger flashed in her eyes, wiping away any confusion that might have been there. "I certainly do. Everybody deserves a private life."

"Including me? Because I have a date myself tomorrow night. If you're not going to be here, we'll have to dig up a baby-sitter somewhere."

She lifted her chin and glared at him. "As it just so happens, I *do* have a date. Start digging."

She marched past him and up the stairs. Dusty watched the sway of her hips, madder than hell because he wasn't carrying her up those stairs in his arms.

She was driving him crazy.

He closed his eyes for a moment, wanting the anger instead of the painful feelings bubbling beneath. Now he'd have to find a baby-sitter; then he'd have to find something to do, so Mimi'd think he was out having a good time. Son of a bitch!

But first he had to get the sight of her out of his head: the sight of her leaning forward to kiss another man, the sight of her with the word "bed" on her lips, the sight of her walking away from him, as if she didn't realize how starved for her he was. . . .

Moving woodenly, he turned out the lights and slowly climbed the stairs. It was going to be a long, cold night.

MIMI SAT on the velvet-upholstered sofa in the living room, cradling Danny in her arms. Tugging gently on his toes, she told him all about the little piggies to the accompaniment of his delighted giggles.

The front door opened and J.D. rushed into the parlor, followed by Dusty.

"Hey, Mom, Dusty wants to take us for pizza!" J.D. cried. "That is—" he glanced over his shoulder at the lanky figure behind him "—if you don't have a date."

"Subtle." Mimi raised one skeptical brow at Dusty. He gave her an ingenuous smile and shrugged. She glanced down at her full-skirted black cotton dress with its bright, appliquéd Mexican embroidery in shades of aqua and red. "Actually I did have a date."

"Past tense?" Dusty sounded hopeful.

"Past tense." It'd been more than a week since her first date with Max and she'd seen him two more times. Tonight they'd planned on a movie, but he'd strained a muscle in his back and had to cancel. "But what about you?" she asked Dusty sweetly. "You've been going out more than I have."

"For you I'll cancel," he said.

It took her a moment to realize he was teasing. Even so, she was pleased. An evening with the five of them at the local pizza parlor sounded like the kind of family outing she'd always enjoyed. Only it was just the four of them; Morrissy begged off.

"My rheumatiz is actin' up," he said. "You young folks run on and have fun. You can bring me leftovers, if'n you don't get the kind with rabbit bait all over it."

"We'll get salami and sausage and stuff like that," J.D. promised, following his own desires as much as Morrissy's.

"And all go into cholesterol arrest," Mimi grumbled. But when they outvoted her at the pizza parlor, she gave in gracefully. "Just this once," she rationalized, adding, "three little words that can get you into a world of trouble!"

"Yeah," Dusty agreed. "Those three-word combinations can be murder."

She gave him a startled look and turned to Danny. He looked adorable in miniature denim jeans that sagged beneath his round little belly and a yellow gingham shirt—like a little cowboy. He seemed happy enough to sit in the high chair while Mimi fed him strained peaches, at least until the pizza came. Then he grew restless.

Fortunately there were no other diners, although the restaurant was doing a brisk pickup business. At least no one else would be disturbed by Danny's fussiness, Mimi thought as she tore off a thick chunk of crust and offered it to him to chew.

"Won't he choke?" Dusty sounded alarmed.

"Not on something that big," Mimi said confidently. "He doesn't have enough teeth to bite off a piece small enough to choke on."

Danny gummed his crust with much enthusiasm. When he dropped it onto the floor, J.D. tossed him a scowl and a replacement crust, then reached for still another slice.

"This is some dynamite pizza," the boy announced, folding his slice in half lengthwise and lifting it to his mouth. "You're not quittin' on me, are you, Dusty?"

Mimi smiled. Every day J.D. talked more and more like Dusty and Morrissy. He was picking up not only their accent but their turns of speech. *Well, what's wrong with that?* she asked herself. Better that than the surfer talk or drug jargon he heard all day in school.

Dusty groaned and rubbed one hand over his flat abdomen. "Sorry, partner, but I don't know where you're puttin' all that. You got a wooden leg or something?"

"Huh?"

J.D. and Mimi looked at Dusty in astonishment, then at each other. All of a sudden the boy laughed.

"He means *hollow* leg!" he exclaimed.

Mimi laughed so hard it brought tears to her eyes, but at the same time she felt herself softening toward Dusty. The man knew nothing about babies beyond what she'd taught him. He didn't know how to handle them, he didn't know the nursery rhymes or the games or *anything*.

Dusty shrugged and gave her a whimsical grin. "I was close," he said.

Mimi, dabbing at her wet eyes with a napkin, turned to see if Danny needed anything—and froze.

The baby sat bolt upright in the high chair, his little arms braced on the tray, while his eyes bulged and his mouth formed an anguished O. In horrible silence, he gasped for breath.

"Oh, my God!" Mimi leaped up, knocking over her chair. With shaking hands she clawed at the high chair's tray. Danny gagged, trying to eject whatever was choking him. His lips were blue.

J.D. and Dusty sprang to her assistance, but all her horrified attention was centered on the baby's distress. She yanked him up from the high chair and instinctively thrust two fingers toward his gaping mouth.

"No!"

Dusty's voice. Something batted her hand aside.

"He's choking!" she screamed, trying to fight free. "What's the matter with you?"

"Give him to me!" Dusty's voice was a roar. He made a grab for the baby, who was limp in Mimi's arms.

"Dusty, you don't know what you're doing!" she cried. She whirled, trying to protect Danny from this crazed man.

He didn't answer, simply seized her shoulders and shoved her into a chair. In the same motion he snatched the baby from her arms. She jumped up, but he shouldered her aside.

Quickly he pulled down the baby's small jaw and looked inside for any visible obstruction. Finding none, he flipped the slack figure facedown over his forearm, until Danny's chin hung lower than his chest.

With the heel of his hand, Dusty gave the still form four quick but gentle blows between the shoulder blades. Then he flipped the tiny body over and gave him four gentle thrusts to the chest, using only two fingers.

Each second seemed an eternity to Mimi. *Breathe, Danny, breathe,* she prayed as she watched Dusty's calm, precise motions.

She had panicked; oh, God, she had panicked, and now Danny might die because of it. Her stricken gaze met J.D.'s. He swallowed hard and reached out to squeeze her cold hand.

Dusty's face was an iron mask of control. He turned the baby facedown again and counted the blows. "One, two, three . . ."

The small body jerked and shuddered. Mimi cried out silently in hope and fear—*Please, God, please!* A thin wail rose from the slight form and Dusty's shoulders sagged. Very carefully, with hands that shook now that the emergency was past, he turned Danny over and lifted him up. Then Dusty sank into a chair as if his legs could no longer support him.

Mimi sagged against his broad back, sliding her arms around his neck. "Thank you," she sobbed, pressing her face against his cheek and tasting her tears. "Oh, thank you!"

"Don't do that," he said in an anguished voice. He bolted to his feet and thrust Danny toward her. "Take him."

She caught the baby against her breast and sat down, hugging him tight. Danny was good and mad now, not to mention frightened. Bright color suffused his chubby face. Screaming his outrage, his little body was stiff in her arms as she rocked him and crooned words of love.

But all the time she looked at Dusty.

Stone-faced, he leaned against the table with his head hanging. His anguished breathing filled her ears; his entire body trembled.

She could hardly bear it. "You saved his life," she whispered. "Dusty, he's okay. You saved his life."

He didn't answer; she didn't even know if he heard her. With Danny subdued to a hiccuping armful, she leaned toward Dusty, settling her hand on the only part of him within her reach—the front of his right thigh. His muscles convulsed beneath her touch. The pads of her fingers dug into the massed strength. Tension surged between them with the power of an exposed nerve.

Slowly he turned his head, his fabled self-possession gone. He looked exhausted, hair tumbling over his forehead and the lines in his cheeks etched deeper by strain. But it was his eyes that stopped her. She had never seen such bleakness in the eyes of any living person, and it stirred something in her she'd never felt before.

The small, frightened voice of J.D. broke the connection. "It was my fault."

Mimi yanked her hand away from Dusty's thigh. "No, honey," she said. "It wasn't your fault."

"It was. I gave him the crust of my pizza and I guess I didn't clean it off good enough. I mean, maybe there was some pepperoni or something on it that made him choke."

J.D.'s freckles stood out starkly against his pasty skin. "But I didn't do it on purpose!" he cried. "Sure, I don't like him much, but I wouldn't—I wouldn't hurt him!"

How could she comfort her son with Danny in her arms? "Don't blame yourself, honey," she pleaded. "If anyone's to blame, it's me. I shouldn't have . . ."

Dusty had watched in silence. Now he held out his right hand, clenched into a fist. Ever so slowly he spread his fingers. A small, white button nestled on his hard palm.

Just like the buttons on Danny's shirt. Mimi scooted the baby around on her lap so she could check. Sure enough, one button was missing.

"He choked on his own button," Dusty said. His voice sounded rusty, as if it hadn't been used in a long time or as if his throat hurt. "I guess it was the fault of the dumb bastard who bought the shirt."

Relief flooded J.D.'s face, quickly followed by sympathy. Awkwardly the boy patted the big man's arm. "Ah, Dusty . . ." he began.

Dusty turned his head slowly. When she saw his expression, Mimi caught her breath. Some barrier deep inside him had been breached. Here at last was a man capable of love and loss.

For a moment she thought he might haul the boy into his arms, but instead he said, "Let's go home."

WITH GREAT CARE, Dusty eased the baby down and into the crib. Danny sighed and flopped onto his belly, knees drawn up, bottom in the air.

Dusty drew the covers over the sleeping child, his movements clumsy. The spring inside him kept winding tighter and tighter, until he thought he'd explode.

*What if Danny had choked to death?*

*Well, he didn't, so don't think about it.*

*But what if he had? What if you never saw that goofy baby grin again or heard him holler when he's mad or laugh when he bangs a wooden spoon on the floor?*

*What if Lori came back to get him?*

Wild anguish streamed through him. He was no longer in control and it scared him. It wasn't his way to chew on "what-ifs." It was his way to take whatever life offered, without flinching.

But he knew he'd never be able to take it if Lori took Danny out of his life.

MIMI STOOD before the parlor window, staring into the darkness. She couldn't seem to get the awful images out of her mind.

"Want a drink?"

Dusty's voice penetrated her melancholy and she turned, her movements jerky and uncoordinated. "No, thanks. You go ahead."

He shook his head. "I don't think so. The way I feel, I might not stop with one."

She knew what he meant. "Did Danny wake up?"

"No. J.D. okay?"

"Yes. Thanks...for being so understanding with him." She licked dry lips. "Morrissy?"

"Said something about hitting the hay early."

Mimi nodded. Morrissy had been given not only the leftover pizza but a blow-by-blow account of the near tragedy.

Ill at ease, she moved stiffly to a velvet-upholstered chair and sat down, her full skirt spreading around her. Nervously she smoothed the fabric over her knees, looking at him from beneath half-lowered lashes. He seemed different, more human. Vulnerable.

She didn't know if that was good or bad. She only knew it made him more appealing and therefore more dangerous.

Dusty eased himself down onto the ottoman before her chair. His legs brushed hers and she yanked her feet back until they rested beneath her chair, her knees pressed tightly together. He reciprocated by shifting around to find some mutually agreeable space for his long legs. He ended up with his thighs spread, one on either side of her knees, but not touching.

"Let it go, Mimi," he ordered gruffly. "It's over. Everything came out all right."

"No." She was so tense her scalp hurt. "I panicked. I had first aid years and years ago, but I never had to use it. Then when an emergency comes along, I fall apart. I never thought I'd do that."

"Don't beat yourself up about it."

That sounded surprisingly like comfort, which would be completely out of character for him, she thought. "You..." she began. He stiffened as if anticipating a blow. "Y-you were wonderful! How did you know what to do?"

He looked down at his hands, folded between his open thighs. "You told me to open a college fund and take CPR if I wanted to do something for the kid, remember? I figured you probably knew what you were talking about."

Her lips parted in amazement. "You mean..." She leaned back in her chair and gave him a puzzled look. "When did you have time to take a CPR class?"

He shifted awkwardly on the ottoman, looking vastly uncomfortable. "Uhh...I didn't exactly take a class...exactly."

"Then what exactly did you do?"

He tugged at one earlobe and stared down at her knees. "I sort of had...private lessons, I guess you could say. Most of those dates weren't... Well, there's this doctor I used to be...close with and she...Damn it, do I have to draw you a picture?"

"No," she said. "No, you don't."

His mouth tightened. "You mad?"

"Mad?" She didn't care if he'd practiced mouth-to-mouth with Michelle Pfeiffer if it meant Danny's life. Or maybe she did...a little. But she definitely wasn't mad.

She was grateful to him, not angry. She could tell him, but he was not a man who trusted words.

She stood up between his legs. He looked at her with surprise on his face; well, she was surprised herself, but not surprised enough to fight the impulse. It was too strong and she'd been fighting too long.

A melting weakness bent her knees. She sank down, bracing her hands on his thighs. As her knees touched the carpet, his powerful legs tightened convulsively against her sides.

"I'm not mad," she whispered. Deliberately she lifted both hands to stroke his lean cheeks. "I'm grate—"

And the rest was lost in his kiss.

# 8

HE HAD JUST A GLIMPSE of startled brown eyes before her lashes fluttered down. She wrapped her arms around his neck with a sigh and opened her mouth to him.

Gripping her waist with his hands, he lifted her fully into the V between his tensed thighs. He held her there, wrapping himself around her. Through his mouth, his hands, through his long, hard thighs pressing into her sides, he felt her tremble. His own body quickened in response.

Tonight his hunger for her would be satisfied, he thought, moving his mouth urgently over hers. His restless hands skimmed up her ribs and brushed the gentle swell of her breasts . . . hesitated . . . returned to cup one sweet globe.

Night after night, day after day he'd ached for her. Tonight he would have her, and tomorrow he would be free of this obsessive need to possess. Tonight he would bury himself in the creamy depths of her—and tomorrow—to hell with tomorrow.

Even in the throes of passion Mimi harbored no such illusions. *If I let this happen, I'll never be free of him*, she thought, even as she surrendered to his kiss. *But I've got to know . . . I've got to know. . . .*

Know true physical ecstasy, for that was what he promised with his lean, hard body, the drugging rapture of his mouth, the intimate knowledge in his hands. He dropped kisses across her cheek, her jaw, down her throat to the tender curve of her shoulder. The flick of his tongue sent shivers radiating to every extremity, and she caught her breath on a moan.

Her head fell back and she let her arms drop until they curved around his widespread legs. With greedy fingers she massaged the backs of his thighs, needing to touch him, feel as much of him as she could. His muscles contracted and she heard his strangled groan. An answering shudder ran through her.

With one quick motion he pulled the elastic neckline of her dress beneath her breasts. He smoothed his hands over their upper curves and she felt her flesh bloom for him.

But it wasn't enough. It wasn't nearly enough. She leaned more fully into his hands, stretching forward to kiss the side of his neck—and in so doing, leaned also into the V between his thighs, her stomach tight against the heated core of him. His breath escaped in a sharp hiss and he went perfectly rigid. His fierce excitement fed her own.

"That's enough!"

His ragged exclamation didn't stop her, but his hands did, rough on her shoulders as he hauled her erect. She glimpsed his face, primitive and dark with passion, and then he surged to his feet.

He lifted her with one smooth, unbroken motion, sliding one arm around her shoulders and the other beneath her knees. Dizzily she clung to him as he strode into the hall, her full cotton skirt rippling around them.

At the foot of the stairs he halted to look down at her possessively. He wanted to say something; she could see it in his eyes and feel it in the tightening of his hands. But he was not a man of words. With an impatient exclamation he took the stairs two at a time. She clung to him, surrendering to the fantasy.

Because this wasn't real. It couldn't be real—ah, but it was wonderful! It seemed right that he should kick open his bedroom door. She felt the strong, heavy beat of his heart beneath her cheek, and that was right, too.

He laid her upon the bed and dropped beside her. He kissed her, at the same time sliding one hand down to lift the billowing skirt to her waist. He slipped his hand inside the elastic of her panty hose, and a magician couldn't have whisked the wispy covering away with greater finesse.

He rolled on top of her, and she welcomed the weight and substance of him as he rocked between her thighs. His denim jeans created an erotic friction against her bare flesh that tore a little gasp of surprise from her tight throat.

Kissing, touching, pressing together and moving apart as if in some ritualized mating dance, he undressed her. The very ferocity of his hunger seemed to hold him back; such passion must be drawn out to infinite delight.

And delight he found in every part of her—her generous breasts with their dusky-rose nipples, so responsive to his touch; the creamy texture of her skin beneath his rough palms and questing lips; the flare of her hips and the supple curve of her thighs.

Stroking softly, he raised her to a fever pitch. Her head rolled on the pillow as though she was half out of her mind with desire. Pushing herself up a little, she arched her back and allowed his hand unhampered access as her breathing grew labored.

"Not that way!" She collapsed back onto the bed. "Together!"

She lay there shaking, while he threw aside his own clothing. He emerged with the beauty of a ravishing but flawed angel, his strong, hard-boned body marred by such a multitude of scars that it took her breath away.

Or perhaps it was the evidence of his undiminished desire that choked her.

He threw himself onto the bed and reached for her. She came into his arms, her fingers stroking down his smooth chest, following a ridged scar that crossed only a fraction of an inch below his right nipple.

"What hurt you?" she whispered, flicking her tongue across the scar.

He made a strangled sound deep in his throat. "Nothing. Nothing that matters . . . now."

She nipped delicately at his rigid nipple and he held perfectly still, as if afraid any movement on his part would discourage her. With a gentleness that bordered on tickling, she brushed her fingertips across his corded belly and lower.

For a moment he bore her attentions stoically. Warming to her task, she was unprepared when he grabbed her and dragged her up the length of his body so he could look into her eyes.

"This is right," he said in a rasping voice. "Inevitable—I wanted to take you to bed the first time I saw you, and I've wanted you every moment since."

It was hard to keep her mind on his words when he was sliding one knee back and forth between her thighs in a slow, rhythmical motion. "I wanted you, too," she whispered. "But not . . . this way."

The tickle of his fingers as they made a leisurely tour of her back sent chills down her spine. "Oh, yes," he said with certainty. "Exactly this way." Lifting her by the hips, he began to rock her gently back and forth.

Mimi groaned and writhed against him. "That's...not what I meant and you know it. I don't want to join anybody's ... harem."

Holding her by the waist, he rolled over until she lay on her back while he crouched above her. For a long moment he stared into her eyes.

"I'm not a man who likes to share," he said. "As long as we're together, there'll be no one else—for either of us."

He spoke so fiercely that she felt a little thrill of pleasure. Until his meaning sank in: *as long as we're together.* A night, a week, a month? Certainly the word "forever" didn't appear to be in the running.

Which made this wrong, all wrong. If she had the strength, she'd stop it right now. She'd get up out of this bed and show him—but he was kissing her, his hands and mouth gliding over her sensitized skin and leaving hot languor in their wake. He sucked one nipple deep into his mouth. She felt the flick of his tongue and cried out.

So she couldn't stand up and walk away, not even when he paused to protect her. She doubted her legs would support her if she somehow managed to rise from this bed of pleasure.

Then he was poised above her, sliding his legs between hers. She saw the triumph on his face and the hunger. His hand curled around her throat, thumb resting on the pulse at the base. Looking deep into her eyes, he entered her...slowly...inch by throbbing inch, penetrating with a languid grace that dragged a long, low entreaty from her throat. It was as if he'd anticipated this moment too long not to savor it.

He lay heavily upon her for a moment, breathing hard and fast. Then he gathered himself and began to move.

She went with him, wrapping her arms and legs around him and uttering hungry little pleasure sounds. He submerged himself in her, plunging again and again, penetrating to new depths, lifting her to new heights.

Muscle spasms rippled out to every part of her body as bliss spiraled through her. Still, the power of her orgasm took her by surprise. She clutched at him, her nails biting into his shoulders and head arching back on the pillow with the force of a silent scream.

With one final eloquent thrust he met his own fulfillment. For a magic moment their fusion reached a pinnacle of perfection; then he flowed against and into her as sweet rapture overtook them.

They lay in each other's arms while passion ebbed away. After a few minutes, Dusty groaned and rolled onto his side, leaving one hand possessively on the curve of her waist. He looked perfectly relaxed, perfectly satisfied.

He slid his hand up to cup her breast as if he owned it, and her, too. "My God," he said in a strangled voice, "that was ... that was ... I wish I had the words to tell you."

"Try." She needed desperately to communicate with him, to understand why she'd just done something she swore she'd never do—indulge in a one-night stand. Because that was all it could possibly be.

He fondled her breast, rolling the nipple lightly between thumb and forefinger. After a thoughtful moment he said, "I always thought there were only two kinds of sex—good sex and great sex. Now I'm going to have to come up with a third category and I'm no damned good at superlatives." He leaned over and kissed her breast. "You are one hell of a woman, Mimi Carlton."

What had she expected him to say? *I love you?* In a painful flash of insight she knew that was what she would have said to him, had he cared enough to raise the subject. She rolled away and sat up on the side of the bed. Despite the deep satisfaction of her body, she felt like crying—or perhaps because of it.

*Now what?* Dusty wondered. Didn't she know a compliment when she got one? He frowned, wondering what the hell her problem was. She couldn't tell him she hadn't been satisfied. Her pleasure had escalated right along with his; she had not submitted, she had participated.

Remembering, he felt a tightening in his loins. And he had thought that once he had her, her allure would fade! Staring at the graceful line of her back, he realized he was becoming aroused again. Reaching out, he traced the ridge of her spine with coaxing fingers.

At his first light touch she jerked upright, flung one horrified glance over her shoulder and sprang to her feet. "I've got to go," she said in a rushed, unnatural voice. She looked around as if she couldn't remember what had become of her clothing.

"Hey, slow down." He swung his feet over the side of the bed and sat up, shoving his hair away from his face with both hands. He didn't know what the hell he'd said or done to upset her, but he wasn't finished with her yet. Not nearly finished with her. "You can't go anywhere until—"

"That's what you think." She grabbed her dress and yanked at it; it was wrong side out and twisted in a knot. She worked on it, her expression tight and unhappy.

But her body was lush and full of promises it was more than able to keep. Beneath the impact of his knowing gaze, her nipples tightened to hard points. Delicate color swept up her throat and into her cheeks.

"Don't do that!" she cried, turning away to shield her nakedness from him. She shook out the dress and pulled it on with clumsy haste.

Dusty stood up, unconcerned by his nudity. "If I misjudged what just happened here . . ." *Women!*

"You didn't," she said quickly. "But it was a mistake that's not going to happen again."

"A mis—!" He couldn't believe she'd say anything so stupid. "Maybe I should have turned to you and asked, 'Was it good for you, too?' Because I give it a fifty-six on a scale of one to ten."

"That's not the problem." She looked miserable. Her lips were soft and swollen, her hair fell over her shoulders in tangles and wisps, her brown eyes were wide and vulnerable. She looked as if some lucky bastard had just made mad, passionate love to her.

She looked absolutely gorgeous, and the lucky bastard wanted to pick her up and start all over again.

"It's because of what almost happened to Danny," she cried. "Our feelings were too near the surface—oh, damn, that's not entirely it, either." She wrung her hands frantically. "I wanted you . . . to kiss me and hold me. I wanted to share what had happened, my feelings and . . ."

She glanced around wildly, her face tormented. She was frightened, and he knew that fear made people do and say things they didn't always mean. He must not push her too hard, or she might back herself into a corner and feel forced to defend it.

He jerked his head toward the bed. "Actions speak louder than words. If making love isn't sharing feelings, I don't know what the hell is."

"That's a cop-out!"

"Okay. Calm down." If he had to talk, then he'd do his best. He cast about for some way to put his feelings into words—what the hell *were* his feelings? Sweat broke out on his forehead. "It's not just the great sex," he said finally, each word an effort both to find and to force out.

She didn't look as if she believed him. He took a step toward her and she backed away. Her glance slid down his body and stopped at the scar across his chest. He remembered her tongue and hands working on him there and bit back a groan.

"A bull did that," he said in a rough voice.

She jerked her gaze up to meet his, a question in her eyes.

"Horns," he explained. "I was gored. And this . . ." He flexed his left arm and held it out so she could see the scars on the tender inner surface. ". . . I got when my horse went down—broke the bone in three places."

He was talking now just to keep her attention and because physical pain was easier to deal with. She stared as if mesmerized. "You don't have to be crazy to rodeo, but it sure as hell helps. As they say, 'It ain't the money, it's the life.' I've had two cracked vertebrae—horse pinned me in a chute in Oklahoma City."

He ran his hands down his sides; she was watching him with an expression mostly of horror now. "I forget how many cracked ribs. I almost lost a thumb dally roping but that was when I was a kid, before I ever went on the circuit. My collarbone's been busted a time or three. At the national finals one year I broke an ankle, but kept on cowboying with the help of a hell of a lot of tape and fifteen shots of novocaine."

"Don't," she said. "This isn't what I want to hear." She turned away as if she could no longer bear the sight of his flawed body.

*She was going to leave.* He stepped up behind her and put his arms around her, just below her breasts. For an instant she stood unyielding. Then, with a little groan, she slumped against him, her head falling back on his shoulder.

"I thought you wanted to know about the scars." His breath stirring her silky, tousled hair. "I don't usually bore people with the details. Who cares?"

"I didn't turn away because I don't care. I care too much, but I can't let you confuse me. Sex isn't enough, no matter how great it is."

She could feel his smile against the back of her bowed neck, and then he murmured, "You thought it was great?"

She groaned. "You *know* it was great. But it could be better." *It's better with love.*

"You're kidding!"

He turned her to face him. She found it incredibly erotic, standing fully clothed in the arms of a naked man. It made him seem vulnerable and herself seem invincible, a fleeting illusion quickly shattered when he thrust one hand through her hair and clasped the back of her head with steely fingers.

"On the outside chance that you may be right," he said, "let's put your theory to the test."

Their lips met in a kiss of such unbelievable sweetness that it took her breath away. His mouth cherished hers, and her response was instant and electric.

His hands played lightly across her back, moving, touching, exploring. She slid her own arms around him, reveling in the unlimited expanse of bare skin. Her hands roamed over him, cupping the hard curve of his buttocks, sliding up to caress the sinewy back. She could feel hard muscle coil below the smooth surface, flexing and impatient, but bound by her wishes. If she so much as swayed toward the bed, he would have her stretched out on it again before she could say—

"Stop!" She dragged her mouth away and gulped in a deep breath.

"What for? You think it could be better and I don't. Let's find out who's right." He thrust his hips into her, letting her feel his arousal while he watched her for her reaction with heavy-lidded eyes.

She grabbed his forearms and swung them wide so she could step out of his embrace. "You haven't got a clue what I'm talking about." She turned and walked out of his bedroom, closing the door quietly behind her.

For four, five minutes he stood there staring after her, willing her to return.

She didn't.

Swearing, he walked into the big bathroom between his bedroom and the sitting room. She was right; he *didn't* have a clue, not to the mystery of women.

Staring into the mirrored wall, he tried to figure a way out of this physical and emotional morass. Trying to understand a woman was like trying to explain the unexplainable, to know the unknowable.

For a long time he stared into the mirror. And finally, as if by magic, the inevitable answer crept into his mind full-blown.

MIMI THOUGHT she had it pretty much together the next morning until Dusty walked into the kitchen. She took one look at him and her face flushed a bright red. In her embarrassment she knocked a glass of orange juice off the table and then was grateful she had the mess to clean up, since it gave her an excuse to keep her face aimed at the floor.

She managed to avoid him until J.D. had gone to school, Danny had gone down for a nap and Maria had gone upstairs to change the beds. Almost on cue, Dusty appeared in the kitchen doorway and crooked a finger.

"You. Me. Talk," he said.

She knew he was right, but it took every bit of strength she possessed to follow him into the parlor and watch him close the door. He gestured to a chair.

This time he didn't settle onto the ottoman at her feet, for which she gave silent thanks. Even so, she felt frazzled and at a disadvantage. He gave her his slow, dimpled smile and she tightened her lips and looked away.

"I can see you're not going to make this easy," he muttered.

"There is no way on God's green earth this could be made easy." She spoke with heartfelt conviction. "Look, we have to get a few things straight or I can't stay in this house, not even for Danny's sake. You know I never intended for us to—"

"Wait a minute, wait a minute. This is my meeting. I get to go first." His face set in stubborn lines. "I knew you'd say that. I thought about this all night and I've figured it out."

"Then by all means you go first." She smoothed out her expression and gave him her attention, not even trying to anticipate where this might be heading.

"Okay, here's the deal," he said. "You and me—" he gestured between the two of them with his forefinger "—we're good together, but neither one of us is interested in a one-night stand. Am I right so far?"

"You're right about me. I wasn't so sure about you." Dare she hope someone had heard her prayers last night? She held her breath.

He looked injured. "You cut me to the quick. What I'm proposing is an exclusive, semipermanent relationship, which will provide us both with what we want. My attorney will draw up the papers—it'll all be perfectly legal." He looked very pleased with himself.

She felt pressure build at the back of her skull and the opening beats of a tension headache. She pressed one hand to her forehead. "Let me see if I understand this," she said carefully. "I give you sex—that's what we're talking about, right? And baby-sitting, of course. Sex and baby-sitting—is there anything else?"

He shifted uneasily. "Those are the highlights."

She nodded. "And in return you'll give me . . . ?"

"Whatever you want—cars, jewelry, furs, travel. J.D.'s education." He gestured expansively. "Name it, and if it's within my power, it's yours."

She tightened her lips and stared at him for a full minute, until he was literally squirming. Then she said one word. "Marriage."

He recoiled. "I never mentioned—"

"No, you didn't." She stood up, clenching her hands into fists. "Do you realize how complicated you're making all this? It'd be much simpler just to get married—not that I would, even if you got down on your hands and knees and begged me!"

"That's a considerable relief, in case I ever go completely loco." He exaggerated his usual drawl, but then his tone turned wheedling. "I wasn't trying to insult you. This is the nineties, sweetheart—the 1990s. You're one in a million, but I'm not the marrying kind."

"You were once," she reminded him, "and I was, am, and always will be. I don't care what decade this is—I don't care what century. I'm not that kind of woman."

"Hey, we won't know until we give it a try. Pick a time period—a year? Ten years? If it doesn't work . . ."

"And J.D., what about J.D.?" She paced around the room. "I want my son to respect women, me included."

He looked appalled. "I respect women! I respect the hell out of 'em. I just don't understand them."

She gave him a dark look. "What kind of message would your 'arrangement' send J.D.? And Danny—but I don't suppose that would be a problem, since his mother will be back for him any day now."

"Maybe, maybe not." Dusty seemed to be getting her message at last; this simply was not something she'd consider. His expression hardened and he made an impatient gesture with one hand. "You don't have to beat me up just because I want you in my life—"

"Not to mention your bed."

"Damn right! My life *and* my bed. I like you and I like your boy, but I don't love you and you don't love me. The truth is, I wasn't any damned good at marriage. You think I've got scars on my body? That's nothing compared to the scars here." He poked one finger at his temple.

"Oh, Dusty, I'm sorry." She clutched her hands together behind her back to keep from reaching out for him. "But not all women—"

"No? You couldn't prove it by me."

They had reached an impasse. Mimi stood up. "You can't have your cake and eat it too," she said tiredly, "not when I'm the cake. You lay one more hand on me and I'm out of here. From now on it's strictly business. Is that clear?"

"Perfectly clear." He started toward the door.

"And Dusty . . ."

He hesitated but didn't turn around.

She spoke very softly but with great certainty. "You really do want a wife. You just don't have the guts to admit it."

"I've got guts I haven't even used yet," he said. He walked out of the parlor. Thirty-two seconds later, he stuck his head back inside long enough to add, "And I apologize for insulting you."

"THAT WAS A WEEK AGO," Mimi told Gloria. "I've barely seen him since."

"Hmm." Gloria nodded.

"Yes?" Desperate for guidance, Mimi leaned forward. On the floor at her feet, Danny gurgled and cooed.

Gloria's eyes gleamed. "Was he good in bed?"

"Gloria!" Mimi pantomimed a tumble from her stool. "I never said we—"

"How was I supposed to interpret the phrase 'got carried away'?"

"You were supposed to pretend you didn't notice."

Gloria waved her sputtering sister silent. "Actually, sleeping with him may not turn out to be so dumb. He obviously enjoyed the sample. Maybe there's still a chance he'll marry you if that's the only way he can get you."

"He won't. And I wouldn't have a man I had to trick." Although, Mimi admitted to herself, she loved this particular man enough to have him under just about any other circumstances, as long as he came with a marriage license. She bent down, picked up a baby rattle from the floor and shook it for Danny.

"Drat!" Gloria tapped long fingernails on the tabletop. "He was far and away your best prospect. Max is okay but Dusty has it all—looks, money..."

"He'd have it all if he was ugly and didn't have a dime," Mimi said unhappily. "He's really wonderful, Gloria, in so many ways. He's kind and generous and so good with the children. But he's simply incapable of trusting a woman. If you can't trust, I don't see how you can love. No, he'll never remarry—I'm sure of it."

"I'm not." Gloria cocked her head to one side. "Maybe if you make him jealous? It's worth a try, girl. You have to think about your future and J.D.'s. How is my favorite nephew, by the way?"

Mimi's shoulders slumped. "That's another problem. He's so happy I get depressed just watching him. He follows Morrissy around like a puppy dog and looks at Dusty as if he could walk on water. He's even been willing to tolerate Danny since the pizza incident."

"I'm not liking the sound of this."

Mimi groaned. "You don't know the half of it. I . . . I think I've . . . fallen in—"

"Stop! I'm going to pretend I didn't hear that. Sweetie, there's no future in a *liaison*. We've got to get you safely married."

Safely married? Could she ever be safe from Dusty?

Later, driving down the road with Danny snoozing beside her in his car seat, Mimi tried to think rationally.

There was always Max. Max was kind, attentive, understanding and apparently content to accept whatever part of her life she was willing to share. As relations with Dusty became more and more strained, she found herself willing to share more and more with Max. This, in turn, increased the consternation of those left behind, nor was it fair to Max.

The circle was growing more vicious all the time.

OVER THE NEXT FEW DAYS Mimi fought to keep her distance from Dusty, but it wasn't easy. Every time she turned around, he'd do or say something so endearing that she'd have to literally walk out of the room to keep her resolve from melting.

Hardest to resist was his developing relationship with the two boys. Walking down the stairs Friday afternoon, she heard the murmur of his voice in the parlor and knew from the tone that he was playing with Danny. She couldn't resist just a peek inside....

Danny, all smiles, lay on his back on the floor with Dusty crouched beside him. The man had a hand on each baby arm, one held up and the other down.

Dusty was chanting in a singsong voice, "This is your rifle, this is your gun. This..." He stretched Danny's right arm higher into the air. "... is for fighting, and this..." He guided the baby's left arm down until his hand patted his diaper. "...is for fun."

"Dusty!" Mimi choked back laughter and tried to look stern. "What are you teaching that baby?"

He looked up quickly, caught red-handed, as it were. "I don't know that stuff you're always telling him about little piggies and bumblebees," he muttered defensively. "I'm teaching him Marine stuff."

"I didn't know you were a Marine." There was so much she didn't know.

"I didn't know you were expecting what's-his-name so early," he countered. His disapproving glance swept over her, taking in the brown slacks and beige silk blouse. With an exaggerated sigh he pulled Danny upright. "Don't worry about the kids." He gave her a long-suffering look. "They'll be fine. You just have a good time."

"I intend to," she said evenly.

She stood there with a frown on a face made for smiles. He hadn't received many of her smiles of late, although sometimes he'd find her playing with the baby or talking to J.D., and for a minute it'd be almost the way it was before . . .

J.D. galloped in, carrying his stamp paraphernalia. "Look, Mom," he ordered. "Dusty replaced those stamps Boy Blunder messed up. I thought maybe you'd help me—"

He stopped short and his eyes narrowed as they took in her appearance. "Don't tell me you're going out again?"

"You know I am," she said, striving for patience. "We can work on your stamps this weekend."

He was shaking his head before she got the words out. "Forget it. Maybe Dusty will help me."

Before Dusty could respond, the door knocker sounded. With a warning glance, she went to answer it.

Dusty watched her walk away; it almost seemed as if the room dimmed without her presence.

HE DIDN'T DELIBERATELY decide to wait up for her; not this time. It just worked out that way.

He was restless, that was all, so restless that he rounded up the kids and Morrissy and drove into town for a visit to the I Scream-You Scream Ice Cream Parlor. And the road to town just happened to lead past Max Renfrew's big Spanish-style estate on a hill overlooking Westbrook. Well, the road led past if Dusty took the scenic route, a mere five or six miles farther.

But hey, it was a beautiful February evening, if you ignored just a little bit of drizzle, so why not? He found out why not as he drove past—Max's car was parked out front. Which meant, just as he'd feared, that Mimi was inside, doing God only knew what with that—

Dusty stepped on the gas. "Banana splits!" he yelled. "Sky's the limit!"

But he was thinking, *What do I have to do to get her back into my bed? What in the hell do I have to do?*

He hadn't come up with any answers by eleven-thirty, when he heard the crunch of tires in the driveway. Torn between anger and relief, he turned toward the stairs just as the telephone rang.

He hesitated with his foot on the first tread, glancing toward the front door, feeling uncharacteristically indecisive. He didn't want her to think he was spying on her, but it was his house. He was under no obligation to make himself scarce for her benefit.

He walked into the library, deliberately leaving the door wide open to guard against some vague, unformed dread that Max would come inside and put his arms around Mimi and proceed to . . . what? He was being ridiculous. She had him tied up in knots because she was the best—

He grabbed the telephone receiver and snarled, "Yes?"

There was a moment of silence. Crank call, Dusty decided—but then his scalp tightened and a warning flashed through him. "Hello?" he said, his voice guarded this time.

He heard a soft intake of breath on the other end of the wire, then a frightened voice whispered, "Daddy? Daddy, it's me, Lori."

# 9

"LORI!" Caught off guard, Dusty had no chance to censor his reaction. There was a moment's electric silence, and then he heard a muffled sob.

"I know it's late—I didn't mean to call until I could tell you I was coming to get my baby. But I just m-miss him so much."

"Where are you?" He felt cold, as if he were encased in a block of ice, but he thought he'd managed to speak with reasonable civility.

"I can't tell you that. I'm sorry."

His scalp tightened at her evasive answer. "Then why did you call?"

"I . . . I had to make sure Danny's safe." A slight hesitation, and then, "He is, isn't he?"

"Danny's fine." Dusty knew he wasn't giving her the assurance she needed, but his resentment went too deep. What did she think she was doing, dumping her kid off with a virtual stranger and then calling up weeks later for a progress report? She was damned lucky he'd talk to her at all.

"I guess he's asleep."

"Yes."

Another long pause. Then she whispered, "Does . . . does he miss me at all? We've never been separated overnight before, not since he was born. I was afraid maybe he wouldn't . . . you know, eat, or that he'd cry a lot. . . ."

"He eats like a horse and hardly ever cries. Lori, you can't get away with this."

"Get away with what?"

"Dropping that little guy off like a bag of dirty laundry when you get tired of him or find him inconvenient."

"I never—"

"No?" He shifted the telephone receiver from one ear to the other. "What, then?"

"I can't tell you. I will when I can, I promise."

"When will that be?"

"I don't know. Soon. I didn't leave him because I didn't want him with me, I had to do it. For his sake."

"Damn, are you in some kind of trouble? If you are..."

"Not like you mean! Please, Daddy, tell me about Danny. D-do you like him?" Her voice sounded pitifully eager. "I hoped you would. I know you were always disappointed because I wasn't a boy, so I thought—"

"What in the hell are you talking about? I never said that." He'd never even thought it.

"Oh, but Mama—never mind, that's not important. All that matters is that Danny's safe and happy. He is, isn't he?"

"You keep using the word 'safe.' Lori, if you're in trouble, why didn't you come to me? Why didn't you let me help you?"

"*I don't want to talk about me!*" Her shriek pierced his eardrum. "I want to know about Danny."

"Then get your butt back here and see for yourself! If you need money, tell me where to send it, but come. Otherwise I'll make my own plans for the baby's future, and they may—" the sound of a handset slamming down interrupted his impassioned speech, but he finished his thought, anyway "—or may not include you."

He stood there for a long count, until his fingers began to ache. Then, very calmly, he hung up.

"Dusty?"

He started violently at the sound of Mimi's voice behind him. He didn't know when she'd come into the room, or if she was alone. He forced himself to turn.

She stood just inside the doorway and there was no sign of Max Renfrew. Dusty didn't know how much she'd heard, but from the alarmed expression on her face it must have been plenty.

She looked at the telephone. "That was Lori."

"Yes."

"She wouldn't tell you where she is or when she's coming back?"

"No."

"And you lost your cool."

He groaned, throwing his head back and closing his eyes for an instant. "She was crying. I made matters worse. But damn it, what kind of mother abandons her kid?"

Mimi walked toward him, her face soft with sympathy. "I don't know Lori or anything about her *except* that she loves her baby. And since you love him, too, it looks to me as if it would be in Danny's best interests for his grandfather and his mother to at least be civil to each other."

"I don't love anybody. If you think I do, you're a fool." Dusty could feel the muscles in his face tense, feel the familiar pressure start to build.

He expected her to respond with anger, but she didn't. Instead she stopped before him. "Poor Dusty," she said. "Hoist with your own unforgiving petard."

"Again." He added that one word like a confession, knowing it was true. He opened his arms and she stepped into them, as if she'd been waiting for the invitation. He gathered her close, pressing her head beneath the curve of his chin.

After a moment he felt her arms slide hesitantly around his waist and she relaxed against him. Her muffled voice drifted up. "I didn't mean to eavesdrop on your conversation, but the door was open."

"It's okay." He began to stroke her shoulders with one hand, while the other pressed against the small of her back. "Maybe . . . maybe I'm glad you heard."

"That's because you need to talk about this. I'm here, Dusty. Talk to me. It'll help, I promise."

He kissed her soft, strawberry-blond curls. "I want to," he admitted at last. "I need to make sense out of all this. I'm just not sure I can."

She turned her head, and he felt her lips brush the skin exposed by the V of his shirt. He wasn't sure if it was accidental or premeditated, but whichever it was, it affected him mightily.

"Try," she said in a low voice. "It's important."

He let her lead him to the cushioned couch built into an alcove at one end of the library. Drapery on both sides added a feeling of intimacy. She sat down amid a multitude of tasseled and fringed cushions and looked up at him expectantly.

This room had always seemed to suit Dusty more than the rest of the house, with its masculine air enhanced by an abundance of leather-bound books and polished woodwork. But it didn't suit him now. She eased into the nest of pillows, lifting one to hug it against her chest.

She wanted to make this easier for him, but didn't know how. He stood before her, his raw-boned face taut and his long, hard body coiled.

"What are you thinking?" she finally asked.

"That this all began a long, long time ago. . . .

"I was a senior in high school when my mother married Mr. Chalmers," Dusty began. "He moved us here to this house, which was okay—I wasn't too crazy about it, but I liked the house better than I liked him. He wasn't any too fond of me, either."

He stopped pacing and his blue eyes took on a look of bitter regret. "One time when Mr. Chalmers was mad at me for one thing or another, my mother took me aside and told me to back off. Talked about how lucky she was at her age to have found a husband who could take care of us."

This story had a horrible, familiar ring. "Maybe she was doing the best she could," Mimi suggested.

"Anything's possible." He hesitated. "I suggested she might have married him strictly for the bucks."

"That was an awful thing to say." Mimi, her own conscience not exactly spotless, stared down at the paisley pattern on the cushion she clutched to her breast.

"Was it?" He tilted his head to one side. "Mother didn't bat an eye. Said she married once for love and once for money, and it evens out. Then she advised me not to force her to make a choice." He chuckled bitterly. "Hell, she did me a favor. At least I knew where I stood."

Which was very much alone. Dispassionately he explained to Mimi that by the time he'd graduated from high school, his mother and stepfather had become obsessed with having a child of their own. That was a particular joy Harry Chalmers had never known, although he'd been married twice before. No one had seemed particularly concerned when Dusty announced he was heading back to Montana.

"Funny how things work out," Dusty said. "They never did have that baby. When Mr. Chalmers died, he left everything to her, including this place. When she died, she had no one to leave it to but me. I guess in the end, I won by default." A muscle in his jaw jumped. "I'd rather have had her love than her money."

"Dusty, all this . . ." Mimi gestured around the room. "Didn't it ever occur to you that this *was* her love? There are plenty of places people can leave their money—charities, monuments. When she left everything to you, she was trying to tell you something."

Maybe later that would make sense to him. Right now he was again that lonely, penniless boy knocking on Morrissy Swain's door. Morrissy had taken him in, of course. A week later he'd met Melinda Conover.

"Melinda worked at the Bar None, which really was a bar, not a ranch," he said. "She was the sexiest thing I'd ever laid eyes on . . . five or six years older than me chronologically, but decades older in experience. One week after we met, we . . . got together. I was a goner."

"You were young." Mimi tried to ignore a surge of jealousy.

"I was in love, or thought I was."

He'd proposed to Melinda every time they'd gone to bed, which had been often. She'd laughed and put him off. When he'd pushed too hard, she'd made it clear that a cowhand was fine for a quick roll in the hay, but she needed a hell of a lot more than that before she made any commitments. He'd been able to see her point even then.

"I needed to make some money," Dusty said with a shrug. "That's when I hit the rodeo circuit the first time. I was so hungry I did it all—roping, riding events. Didn't take me long to get the hang of it. I was saving every penny I could get my hands on, and then Melinda suggested that she open a joint account for 'our' savings."

"Oh, Dusty, you didn't!"

"Didn't I? Six months later I went back for her and she . . ."

"Was gone."

He raised his brows, mocking himself. "Have I told you this story? She'd cleaned out the bank account and skipped two days earlier. She left a note. . . ."

Sorry about this, but I need a man, not a boy. If you love me, you'll understand. . . .

He'd understood, all right. He'd started drinking in the Bar None, and five days later they'd poured him onto a bus to Helena, where he'd joined the Marine Corps.

His choice had turned out to be a good one—women loved the uniform. His four years in the Corps had passed pleasantly enough. Discharged at twenty-two, he'd drifted back into rodeo.

The Suicide Circuit he'd called it, and that had been how he'd played it—drinking too much, partying too much, fighting too much—and sleeping with too many women. He'd entered every event in sight, always on the go.

Then he'd met up with Melinda again.

"I found out later she'd been married at least once before I ever met her. She'd left the Bar None to marry again—a beer delivery man, I think it was. She left him to marry me.

"A year down the pike she left me to marry someone else." But before she'd left, she'd given birth to a daughter.

He whirled and crossed to a big globe perched on its own polished wooden stand. He rested his hands on it for a moment, then set it spinning with a sharp, violent twist of his wrists.

Mimi watched him, hurting for him. "Did she tell you the baby wasn't yours?"

He gave her a quick, narrow-eyed glance. "Yeah."

"But surely you didn't believe her!"

"Not at first . . . then I did, and then—hell! What was I supposed to think?"

"That your ex-wife was a vicious, vengeful woman. Dusty, I've never seen Lori, but her son is your grandson and I'd stake my life on it. My gosh, have you looked at that baby's eyes? They're yours!"

"You think so?" He frowned as if hope were a stranger, then shrugged. "Whatever—I finally got Melinda's message. She'd do whatever was necessary to get shed of me. There were other things, too. . . ."

"What other things?"

He turned toward Mimi. She'd stacked cushions at one end of the couch and half reclined on the rich pile of fringe and tassels.

Looking at her, all peaches and cream and warm, smooth female flesh, he felt himself grow hard and hot. All other women, past and present—even Melinda—paled by comparison. He licked his lips and let his gaze slide down the length of Mimi's rounded body. "I want to make love to you," he said, surprised to discover how dry his mouth was.

She caught her breath and her eyes narrowed. "No, you don't. You want to have sex with me. There's a difference."

"To you, maybe." He crossed the space between them and knelt, but didn't touch her. Looking into her eyes, he struggled to understand what he was feeling.

He did not love this woman, he assured himself, but he wanted her. She had aroused an ache in his gut that he feared would never be permanently eased. He wanted her for the long term; he wanted her committed to him and him alone. He didn't want to share her and he didn't want to be uncertain of her.

There was only one way to accomplish all that and he damned well knew it. But marriage? Could it work for him instead of against him?

He did not love this woman, but he loved the way she made him feel: important, fascinating, admired . . . special. He loved sex with her—okay, he loved sex, period, but with her the act took on new dimensions and an emotional intensity unlike anything he had ever experienced—no, not even in the early days with Melinda.

Again he heard the old refrain ringing in his ears, familiar as a broken record: *What do I have to do to get her back into my bed—permanently?* This time he acknowledged the answer: *Marry her.*

"What are you thinking?" Her lashes fluttered down as if to conceal her expression.

"That I'm going to make love to you right here and right now." He stood up and crossed to the big double doors, swinging them closed with a decisive snap.

Mimi sat bolt upright among the cushions, her breath coming in anxious little gulps. "No, Dusty," she began in a warning tone. "I told you I won't—"

"I heard you. I tried to respect your feelings, but I think you've changed your mind." He walked back to stand before her. He yanked his shirttail free and went to work on the buttons, his attention never leaving her face.

"Don't look at me that way," she begged breathlessly. "You make me feel . . ."

"What? How do I make you feel?" He ripped off his shirt and dropped it to the floor. Stepping forward until his knees pressed against the front of the couch, he leaned forward, caught her by the elbows and lifted her against him.

She shook her head, her eyes stormy, but she didn't fight him or try to pull away.

Dusty kissed her cheek. "Scary, isn't it? Putting your feelings into words is harder than telling somebody else to do it. But that's okay. I know how you feel."

"You don't," she denied. She rolled her head away and only succeeded in giving him unhampered access to the side of her neck. "You couldn't."

"I do. I feel the same way. We've both been waiting for this, ever since the last time."

"The last time *was* the last time!" she cried. "Don't do this to me, Dusty, don't!" She pressed her palms against his bare chest, her nails scratching lightly across his skin. His muscles leaped uncontrollably. "The only relationship I'm interested in is a permanent one. What would I do when you get tired of me?"

"What makes you think that'll happen?" he countered, and crushed her lips with his.

She twisted her arms around his neck and surged to meet him. His mouth, hot and ardent, tempted hers to open. He stroked his hands up and down her sides, his body bearing down, forcing her back, back, back....

She toppled over, pulling him down with her into the soft welter of cushions. His weight was a burden she welcomed. She slid her fingers beneath the waistband of his denims and hung on, swept away on a wave of desire.

His mouth sought the smooth skin of her throat, while his hands fumbled with her buttons. His voice flowed around her like honey. "I want to stay here forever."

*Forever.* Not semipermanently, she thought, giving in to the undiluted hunger coursing through her. He pulled her blouse wide and pressed his lips to the curving slope of her breast. The hook of her bra offered little resistance, and he nuzzled that last flimsy obstacle aside.

He flicked his tongue across one nipple while he played with her other breast, kneading and lifting. He seemed to know exactly how to arouse her, or maybe . . . maybe anything he did would be equally effective, she thought foggily, because he was the one doing it. She threaded her fingers through his hair and lifted her torso, offering herself. At last he sucked a taut nipple fully into the hot moistness of his mouth and she couldn't stop the exclamation that escaped her lips. "Oh, yes!"

She writhed beneath his hand as he slid it down her stomach to curve between her thighs. Her muscles contracted in rapturous anticipation that was quickly rewarded. The motions of his hands, his mouth and tongue, sent shudders of desire ripping through her.

With her own hands and mouth she sought him, moving restlessly, withholding nothing, seeking the friction of his body on hers, around hers.

In hers. She wanted him inside her, filling her, possessing her. She wanted to belong to him in every way a woman could belong to a man. With him she wanted to confront the ultimate mystery of the universe . . . the mystery of love.

And she wanted it forever, heaven help her. If he rose now and walked away and she never saw him again, she'd still belong to him and he to her. He might refuse to acknowledge love, but he took her with love. She felt it in his every touch, in every taste and texture, in every glance of those compelling blue eyes.

And she loved him. She loved him! That silent acknowledgment brought a sweet burst of laughter to her lips. Dusty raised his head, still holding her nipple between his lips. The slight tugging motion sent new excitement coursing through her. His eyes asked a question.

She caught her breath and gave him a misty smile. His pupils dilated; watching him, she felt a kind of craziness flash through her.

"I love you," she said. "I really do love you."

Tears of relief sprang into her eyes and she closed them, sagging back onto the pillows. It had been a terrible burden, carrying that secret around inside her.

She wasn't even sure her words had registered, for he didn't acknowledge her confession. It didn't matter. She knew. She had never been so happy; she started to laugh, but he stopped the sound with his mouth.

Their hands moved with a single mission, unzipping, unbuttoning, tugging.... Pillows tumbled to the floor, clothing flew through the air. Slim, smooth arms and legs, strong, muscular arms and legs met, entwined, embraced. Bodies twisted and turned, seeking, rubbing in the most erotic motions.

Panting with excitement, she opened her eyes and stared into his. He gave her a smile of piercing sweetness. Before she knew what was happening, he'd caught her by the waist and rolled over, hauling her on top. Her thighs slid apart and she straddled him.

At the first touch of his hand, a wild, sweet frenzy shot through her and she gasped. Her breathing grew labored as he explored, teased, built a craving for that which he deliberately withheld.

But his control was not infinite. She saw the struggle in his face and heard it in his own ragged breathing. She was ready, more than ready. All he had to do was show her what he wanted, and at last he did.

"Like this?" she whispered.

"Yes. Oh, yes, just like that."

He lifted her by the waist and held her while she positioned herself above him. Carefully he probed her slick, sultry flesh, his muscles quivering with heroic control.

"Now?"

"Yes! Now—"

Grasping her securely by the hips, he brought her slamming down to meet the thrust of him. He surged into her—impaled her. She gasped and closed her eyes. Her head fell forward as he filled her, possessing her more completely than she had dreamed possible.

She wanted to weep with the beauty of this fusion, but he was moving, driving into her. His hands rose to cover her breasts. She leaned into that support, her own hands closing around his wrists. He invaded her more deeply and more profoundly with every rhythmic stroke, each eliciting a soft gasp.

Her accelerating pleasure seemed too sweet to be endured. His ultimate penetration sought and found the very core of her. His body convulsed beneath hers; time stopped and glory burst inside her. Floating free in a realm of pure sensation, a low, astonished sound burst from her throat. Surely her heart would burst with the joy of sharing this wild rapture.

She fell forward into his arms and lay there stunned. Her mind still reeled as the final vibrations faded. "Oh, my gosh," she said in an incredulous voice. "Oh, my gosh!"

He stroked her back and hips and kissed the top of her tumbled curls. He sighed, a long, satisfied sound. After a while he said carefully, "At the risk of putting my foot in my mouth again—which wouldn't be easy, considering the position I'm in . . ."

She lifted her head from his chest so she could look at him. His lean cheeks were flushed and a pulse throbbed in his throat, but what struck her most was how defenseless he appeared. "Yes?" she encouraged.

"Would you tell me about your husband?"

"D-David?" She rolled over and snuggled into the curve of his shoulder, her mouth dry as cotton. "What do you want to know?"

After a long hesitation he asked, "Did you love him?"

"Yes. Oh, yes." She closed her eyes, remembering. "We grew up together. He was the only boy I ever loved."

Again the long, uneasy pause. "If you don't mind me asking, how did he die?"

"A brain tumor killed him." She shivered and nestled closer, seeking comfort. He responded by wrapping his arms even more tightly around her. "For two years he...I...we..."

"Shh." He cupped the back of her head with his hand and held her tenderly until the tremors passed. "You stuck it out for two years," he said. "That's really something."

"It wasn't *something*. I loved him. When I became his wife, we made a promise—in sickness and in health."

"A lot of people make promises they never intend to keep. A lot of people say whatever they have to, to get what they want."

"I don't!"

"You sure?"

She struggled around until she could rise on one elbow to look down at him. "What are you getting at?" she asked. "What do you want from me?"

His struggle was there on his face. "What do I want from you?" A muscle in his jaw jumped. "I want to make love to you without using a damned condom. I want your undivided attention and I want to give you mine—

anything you want, anything I want. I want to be sure of you, damn it."

She heard him with growing outrage. "In other words, nothing's changed."

"Everything's changed."

"Ha!" Through a haze of anger she saw the tightness of his face. Well, she didn't care, not anymore. He'd had his chance. "Have I told you lately what you can do with your exclusive, semipermanent relationship? You can take that sucker and—"

"Shut up and let me finish." He grabbed her by the shoulders and shook her. "I've given up on that. You already turned it down."

"Then what was this, my farewell performance?" The knife in her breast twisted cruelly; she spoke harshly to hide the hurt. She tried to pull back, but he merely tightened his grip on her shoulders. "Let me go!" she demanded, voice quivering.

"Not until you let me finish."

Her struggle was both brief and pointless. He held her easily and simply waited for her to calm down. When she did, he spoke in a voice as rough as sandpaper.

"Mimi," he said, "would you be interested in marrying me?"

# 10

MIMI SHOVED AWAY from Dusty and sat up. "That's not funny," she cried. Her tone didn't carry enough conviction to suit her, so she said it again with more force, "Damn you, that's not funny!"

"Am I laughing?" In fact he looked downright grim. He rose on one elbow, leaned forward and kissed her bent knees, one after the other. "I'm dead serious. I can think of a million reasons why this is the right thing to do, beginning with what just happened here."

"Sex isn't enough," she said, wishing it were.

"Maybe not, but it's a hell of a good start." He rubbed her knee slowly, tracing its curves with his hand. "Look, with palimony the way it is today, why balk over a piece of paper? In a practical sense it doesn't make any difference."

"It makes a big difference to me!"

He nodded. "I know. I don't understand, but I know." He grimaced. "Cut me some slack here, will you? I'm trying to be sensitive to your feelings."

*Sensitive!* She stared at him, wondering whether she should hit him or kiss him, laugh or cry. He shifted uneasily, picking up a cushion that he tortured out of shape between his strong hands. Not for the first time it occurred to her that he might care more for her than he would admit—maybe more than he even knew.

If there was a chance that he could ever love her, she'd marry him in a minute. Her heart leaped, then settled into a wild drumming. She leaned forward and placed her hands upon his shoulders.

"Tell the truth," she ordered in an unsteady voice. "Do you love me?"

He blinked. At once she understood this was a question he had both anticipated and dreaded. "Would you believe me if I said I did?" he asked warily.

She thought for a minute. "Yes," she decided. "Know why?"

His brows rose in the equivalent of a shrug. "Because you're gullible?"

She shook her head slowly. "Because I love you."

His eyes turned dark and stormy. "You don't have to keep saying that." His voice grated on her nerves. "I've already proposed."

"No. No, you haven't." She lowered her body until her nipples brushed against his chest. "You asked *would I be interested*. Care to rephrase the question?"

He groaned. "You're a hard woman, Mimi Carlton."

"Not as hard as you are." She let her body slide over his until she lay on top of him. She moved against him until he could not doubt her intention. "If you mean it, ask nicely." She rotated her hips, savoring his instant response. She was teasing now—flirting, leading him on. "Bite the bullet, Dusty," she invited. "I'm waiting."

"I'm about to bite something, but it won't be any damned bullet." He parted his thighs and she slipped even more intimately against him. He licked his lips. "Marry me, Mimi," he said in a rush. "Marry me, damn it, before you drive me crazy!"

She could tell him a thing or two about who was driving whom where. She dug her fingertips into his chest, beginning to believe this was really happening. "Okay," she agreed breathlessly, "I'll marry you because I lo—"

He threw his arms around her, and her voice broke off in a squeak as he crushed her against his chest. Much, much later, just as he drifted into sleep, she bent over him and whispered into his ear.

"I *do* love you, Dusty. I love you."

Long after her breathing had become soft and even, he lay there wondering if it could possibly be true.

He finally concluded that it wasn't any too likely.

DUSTY LEANED OVER and kissed Mimi's cheek. She gave him a sleepy smile and slid her arms around his neck, trying to pull him down beside her in the bed. It was not a prospect easily refused.

"No time, honey." Gently he removed her hands and straightened. "It's almost seven, and I promised J.D. we'd get in an early ride this morning."

Her eyes flew wide. He saw the drowsy look of satisfaction fade and concern take its place.

"J.D. I've got to tell him about us."

Dusty pulled on his shirt and stuffed the tail into his jeans. "I'll do it."

"You?" She shoved her tangled hair away from her face. "Shouldn't I be the one? I am his mother."

He turned heavy-lidded eyes upon her. "It's hard for me to believe a wild thing like you is anybody's mother." He sat down and reached for his boots. "It'll be better coming from me."

"Okay, if you think so," she said doubtfully, and then her expression softened. "I can refuse you nothing." Her eyes gleamed wickedly as she repeated, "Nothing!"

He wished he had time to take her, at her word and otherwise. Fortunately there'd be plenty of time later. A lifetime at least. Smiling, he stood up and walked to the door, already anticipating his return.

"Dusty?"

He hesitated with his hand on the doorknob.

"I love you. I'm going to keep repeating it until you believe me."

He grinned a little crookedly. Whether or not he believed her, it was good to hear.

THE WEEKS ON THE RANCH had already begun to change J.D. The boy was filling out. He wasn't nearly as skinny, and his young body was becoming toned and fit from the outdoor life. Dusty watched with unaccustomed pride as J.D. pulled his little bay horse to a stop atop a knoll and grinned over his shoulder.

J.D. was also learning fast. The quick intelligence that often isolated him from his peers helped him absorb knowledge and information at a gallop. In short, he was a pleasure to have around.

Dusty reined in his buckskin, relaxing deep into the saddle. Pastureland and orchards spread out before him, not exactly the wide-open spaces he'd grown up with, but not bad for Southern California. Funny how much more content he'd been with these surroundings lately.

J.D. swung one leg up and hooked a knee casually around the saddle horn. He gave Dusty a self-conscious grin and picked up the conversation where they'd left off back at the barn. "Mr. Swain says if I keep at it, I'll make a roper yet."

"If Morrissy says it, you can take it to the bank."

J.D. nodded agreement. "He says when I get good enough, maybe you'll teach me the dally."

Dusty laughed. "That old reprobate." He held up his right hand and wiggled his thumb. "See that scar at the base there? That's what happens to dally ropers. Throw that rope, take a few turns of the free end around the saddle horn, and if you're not payin' attention you can lose a thumb, unless you're lucky. My advice is, tie the end of that grass rope to the old apple and play it safe."

"Okay, Dusty. Anything you say."

The boy looked at the man with perfect trust and confidence, a trust and confidence Dusty was loath to threaten. Ninety percent sure of the reception his news would receive, there was still always an outside chance that the kid would dig in his heels.

But Dusty wasn't one to put off an unpleasant chore. "J.D.," he said, "can we get serious here for a minute."

"Sure, Dusty. What's up?"

The man shifted in the saddle, leather creaking. "I won't pussyfoot around about this. I'm going to talk straight, man to man."

Alarm flared on the boy's face. "Sure." He hunched his shoulders.

"It's about your mother. She wants to get married and—"

"Ah, no, jeez!" J.D. yanked his leg over the pommel and thrust his foot at the stirrup. His freckled face screwed up. "Don't tell me that! I don't like that Max and there's no way—jeez, I don't need a father!"

Taken aback, Dusty tried to interrupt the tirade. "Hold on, partner. You don't underst—"

"I won't go! You won't make me leave, will you, Dusty? I'll work hard if you let me stay—you won't be sorry!"

The power of J.D.'s emotional upheaval set the little bay dancing sideways. The boy sawed on the reins and the horse sat back on its haunches. With a frustrated yell, J.D. banged his heels into the quivering sides. The animal, a trained roping horse, bounded forward like a jackrabbit.

J.D. lost it. He flipped back over the cantle, ass over teakettle. The bay bolted past and Dusty kept a tight rein on his own horse while the kid landed on the soft green turf, flat on his back.

He lay there stunned, the breath knocked out of him. Calmly Dusty stepped out of the saddle and dropped the reins, effectively ground-hitching his horse. He took his time walking over to J.D., who stared up blankly.

After a few moments, hot color rushed into the boy's pale cheeks and he gulped in a breath. "I won't go and she can't make me!"

"Shut up for a minute and listen." Dusty spoke roughly. Hunkering down, he grabbed a fistful of shirt and hauled J.D. to a sitting position. They glared at each other, eyeball to eyeball. "You don't have to go, boy, not ever. Your mother's fixin' to marry *me*."

It took a while for that to sink in but when it did, the stiffness melted away from the young face. Hope leaped into his eyes. "Do—" His voice cracked and he swallowed hard. "Do you mean it?"

"Hell, yes."

"Then that means you're going to be my... what?"

The boy's unguarded emotions stirred something in Dusty that was completely new. Something that frightened him. "I guess I'll be any damned thing you want me to be," he said, as if it didn't matter to him one way or the other.

A sort of wonder washed over J.D.'s face. "W-will you be my father?"

Dusty stood up, hauling the boy with him by the scruff of the neck. He shook the kid like a puppy and stood him on his feet. "Yeah, but you gotta learn how to ride." Jesus, his voice was cracking like the kid's had. "No son of mine's gonna get piled twice by an old crow bait like that bay."

Tears slid down J.D.'s freckled cheeks. "Ah, Dusty." He choked. Leaning forward, he wrapped his arms around Dusty's waist and buried his face in the man's chest.

For a few frozen seconds Dusty stood there petrified, his hands hanging awkwardly by his sides. Then, very slowly, he enclosed the boy in the safe circle of his arms . . . the safe, loving circle of his arms.

"HEY, LET'S THROW a party to celebrate!" Gloria said when they told her.

Mimi glanced doubtfully at Dusty, but he grinned and shrugged. He'd been so agreeable lately that even Morrissy had noticed.

"Why not?" he said mildly. "Invite everybody—the country club crowd and the spit 'n' whittle crowd. Ought to be interesting."

"When?"

He dropped a kiss onto the tip of Mimi's nose. Now that they were officially engaged and she was wearing his diamond, he seemed much more relaxed. Or—she stifled a satisfied smile—now that she spent every night in his bed.

Gloria waited until Dusty went off to find J.D. and Morrissy before giving vent to her delight. "Did I tell you to make him jealous?" she crowed. "The poor sap didn't stand a chance against the two of us!"

Mimi, shoveling baby food into Danny's sticky face, frowned. "It wasn't that way at all," she protested. "I happen to love him."

Gloria's eyes widened in an approximation of innocence. "Absolutely. It's a well-known fact that it's as easy to love a rich man as a poor man. The important thing is, your birthday wish is about to come true. Your worries are over. Hot damn!"

Danny grabbed the spoon and managed to dump applesauce down the front of his shirt. Mimi swabbed at his chest with a paper napkin. "I never should have told you about that," she griped. "Are you going to sit there and harass me or are you going to help me plan this party?"

"Plan, by all means. Let's see, first we need an appropriate date." Gloria pursed her lips. "How about April Fools' day?"

THEY HELD THE PARTY on the first Saturday in March, in midafternoon. They even decorated the big old Victorian with festive golden bows and garlands of greenery, trying with limited success to keep everything out of reach of Danny's eager little hands.

Maria came in specially that day to assist; she also planned to return for a few hours the following day to help with the cleanup. In the kitchen, she and Mimi worked side by side on miniature tacos and quesadillas and nachos and other goodies.

"I've never seen Señor Dusty so happy," Maria confided, pausing in the process of grating a chunk of cheese. As was her custom, she spoke to Mimi in Spanish. "Now if only his daughter were here for this happy event."

"Yes, if only." Mimi reached for another ball of dough to be rolled into a tortilla. She knew that Lori's continuing absence—her very silence—ate at Dusty like a decaying tooth. Sometimes Mimi caught him staring at his grandson and knew he was really thinking about his daughter.

Sometimes she wondered if he was becoming *too* attached to Danny. She picked up the small Mexican rolling pin. She was sure he was too fine a person to do anything to hurt his own daughter, but he'd dropped a few hints about the baby's future. She'd even heard the dreaded word "custody." On the other hand, if Lori didn't show up soon, what could she expect?

The guests were invited for two o'clock, but Gloria showed up an hour earlier with her own shaker of vodka martinis. "Here's to the blushing bride and the well-connected groom," she sang out. "Cheers!" She drank directly from the shaker.

"Where's Neil?" Mimi figured he was the only person who might be able to take Gloria in hand and calm her down. "I thought he was coming with you."

"Forget Neil! He's nothing but an old party pooper. Now tell me what I can do to help!"

Mimi and Dusty exchanged glances, hers worried and his impassive. She knew he wasn't one to get involved in other people's business. He didn't like offering advice— or taking it, for that matter. He expected to make his own mistakes and let others make theirs.

Later, when she had a moment alone with him, she voiced her concern. "Gloria started drinking before she even got here," Mimi admitted. "She cares a lot more about Neil than she'll admit. I hope this is just a little tiff and not something serious."

"Whatever it is, it's none of our business." He caught her arms and wrapped them around his waist.

"Dusty!" She avoided his kiss, looking around self-consciously. Seeing that they were alone, she gave in, pressing herself against him. "I guess I just want everyone to be as happy as I am."

Both pleased and embarrassed, he tried to make light of it. "If all it takes to make you happy is a party, we can have lots of 'em."

She laughed and kissed him lightly on the mouth. "*You* make me happy, Dusty. I love you."

He'd become accustomed to hearing her say those words, but they never failed to give him a jolt of pleasure. Could it be that he was starting to believe her? Could it be that he was starting . . . cautiously, defiantly, unwillingly . . . to return those feelings?

The kitchen door swung open. J.D. stood there, Danny in his arms and a big grin on his face. "Jeez!" the boy exclaimed with mock disapproval. "Close your eyes, Danny. You're too young to see this." He clapped one hand over the baby's face and edged past, giving the embracing couple a wide berth.

"Fresh kid!" Dusty called after him.

"Happy kid," Mimi corrected. "He loves you, too. You're a lovable kind of guy."

No one, to his knowledge, had ever called him lovable before. Walking down the hall arm in arm with this beautiful and passionate woman, he realized that for the first time in many, many years, he was beginning to believe that perhaps love actually existed. If it did, had he found it at last?


BY FIVE O'CLOCK an overflow crowd of well-wishers had assembled. They spilled out of the parlor into the hall and library.

It seemed to Mimi as if everybody in town must be here—everybody except Neil Gordon. Even Martin and Max had accepted the invitation with good grace. Pete Patterson and the gang from the feed and supply store clustered around Dusty's desk in the library, drinking beer and eating massive amounts of food. All except Hank—Hank played with Danny on the couch at the end of the room.

A couch that held very special memories for Mimi.

Hank grinned at her as she paused before them. "He's grown," he observed, reaching out to give the baby's thigh a gentle tweak. "Look at these drumsticks!"

Danny giggled and bounced up and down among the cushions. He wore a short romper in a bright red knit that made his eyes look even bluer.

"Would you like me to take him now?" Mimi asked. "You must want to get back to your friends."

"Naw. We're doin' fine." He rubbed his bearded jaw. "Thought the little guy's mother might be here tonight."

Mimi gave him a sharp glance, but all she said was a noncommittal "No."

Hank picked Danny up in his arms and rose. "She better make tracks back here, or she'll have ta Indian rassle ol' Dusty to get this little varmint back."

He said it jokingly, but it seemed more an ominous portent to Mimi. Dipping his chin in her direction, he sauntered across the room toward his friends, stopping at the first group he passed to allow them to admire the baby.

Maria slipped into the room and glanced quickly around. Spotting Mimi, she worked her way through the throng. "That sister of yours is making her move," she said in Spanish. "She's got that good-looking blond man backed up in the hall outside the kitchen, and she's all over him."

Mimi groaned. "Good Lord, you mean Martin?"

Maria rolled her eyes. "What can I say?" She stood aside to let Mimi pass.

In the hall, Mimi almost collided with Martin Montgomery. His face was flushed and his shirt was unbuttoned halfway to his waist.

She peered past him, almost afraid to ask. "Is anything wrong?"

"Not a thing," he said too quickly. "Excuse me—I think I could use a drink."

She watched him go, not even noticing J.D. until he tugged on her sleeve. "Ma, I think you'd better do something about Aunt Gloria," he said in a stage whisper.

Almost at the same moment, she heard Gloria's strident voice from the parlor. "Okay, where's the birthday girl? I mean the *bride!*" She laughed drunkenly.

Mimi's heart sank. She found Gloria standing in front of the fireplace—maybe weaving in front of the fireplace was more like it—with everyone in the room looking at her. Dusty stood to one side, watchful but not interfering.

*Gloria, what are you doing?* Mimi started forward and Gloria noticed her for the first time.

"Miriam!" Gloria raised her champagne flute. She glared around at one and all. "Pay attention, here. I'm making a toast!"

The murmur of voices died away and glasses were raised. Gloria uttered a satisfied grunt. "To my sister," she announced, "who's never wanted anything but the best." Her voice was only slightly slurred. "And to her intended, a guy who can finally give it to her."

Mimi groaned and glanced at Dusty. He was watching the proceedings with a slight frown on his face. She forced herself to smile as she made her way to his side. Rising on tiptoe, she kissed his cheek and whispered, "She's had it. I'm going to try to get her to lie down for a while."

"Good idea," Dusty agreed. His puzzled expression never changed.

MIMI AND DUSTY stood on the front steps, waving goodbye to the last of the guests. It was nearly ten o'clock; the party had been fun, but now she was exhausted. With both children already in bed there remained only one final chore.

She leaned close to Dusty's side, comforted by his arm around her waist. "Now all we have to do is wake Gloria and send her on her way. Then, if we're lucky, we can—"

"Gloria's awake."

It was little more than a croak. Gloria stood weaving in the open doorway. She held a water glass in her hand, but Mimi would have been willing to bet the clear liquid inside was not water.

She groaned. "Gloria, don't you think you've had enough of that stuff?"

"What stuff?" Gloria took a deep swallow.

Mimi cast a regretful glance at Dusty. "I'll have to drive her home. There's no way she can get behind a wheel."

"I'll do it."

"Oh, no—" She felt a quick flare of alarm, but why should she? Dusty had known Gloria for years; he certainly wasn't going to cast any stones. "Are you sure? I don't mind doing it."

He smiled, the slow smile she'd hungered for from the first moment she saw him. It came much more frequently these days. "Will you be waiting for me when I get back?"

"Try and stop me."

"Then I don't mind."

He took her into his arms and kissed her with a profound tenderness. She clung to him, her heart overflowing with happiness.

"Sheesh! Can't you two at least wait until I leave?"

Dusty gently set Mimi aside. "Gloria," he said without inflection, "you could be a real pain in the butt with very little effort." He added in an undertone to Mimi, "Don't worry. I'll take her home and be right back."

She clung to his hand, unprepared for the panic she could not explain. "Couldn't Morrissy—?"

He pried her fingers loose. "Baby, he went to bed an hour ago. Thirty minutes, that's all it'll take."

Behind her she heard Gloria's disgusted voice. "Now what the hell did I do with those keys?" and then a crash of splintering glass, as if Gloria had dropped—or thrown—her drink.

Mimi braced herself against a surge of resentment. There was nothing she could do now. This was what she got for not urging Gloria to seek professional help with her drinking problem weeks ago.

GLORIA COLLAPSED into a boneless heap onto the passenger seat of the Mercedes-Benz and let out a gusty sigh. Dusty, turning out of the driveway and onto the road, glanced at her.

"You okay?"

"Why the hell wouldn't I be?"

She flung the words at him like an accusation. He shrugged; he'd seen a few drunks in his day. His policy had always been to let them take care of themselves, right up to the point when they endangered some innocent bystander. Under no circumstances did he argue with them and so he said patiently, "No reason, Gloria."

"Ha!" She gave him a triumphant glance from half-closed eyes, apparently under the impression that she was making sense. "I was the life of the party—wasn't I the life of the party? Did you shee me making time with

Martin What's-his face? Now that Mimi's thrown him over ... Neil's a jerk, so why not?"

She yammered on, slurring her words. Dusty only half listened. After a few minutes she seemed to run out of steam.

Several miles down the road she sat up straight again. "I knew ol' Mimi would get her wish," she announced. "If I told her once, I told her a million times ..."

She swung her head toward the window and pressed her forehead to the glass.

"Told her what?" Dusty couldn't resist asking, anticipating his pleasure at being told that Mimi had got her wish because her wish was him.

"What?"

"You said you told Mimi something a million times."

"Oh, yeah. Her birthday."

"What about her birthday?"

"Oh. Well, this wish." Gloria giggled. "She wished she could shag a millionaire—" She covered her mouth with her hand. "Oops, what I said! She wished she could *snag* a millionaire before she turned forty. She doesn't look thirty-nine, does she! How old do you think I am? C'mon, how old?"

"You're putting me on, right? She set out cold-bloodedly to—?"

"Hell, no! She's hot-blooded, you boob! But David's brain thing wiped them out—he promised her the moon and she didn't get even a teensy-weensy star. She's sick and tired of being poor as Job's turkey. I offered—I'm a good shister, I'm not stingy! But I guess she'd rather earn 'em on her back than take mine." Gloria laughed heartily. "She...she...God, I'm thirsty. Do you think we could stop for a—? No, I guesh not."

Dusty felt as though he'd been blindsided. He tightened his hands on the steering wheel until his fingers ached. "Gloria," he asked, "are you mad at Mimi about something?"

"Mad? Hell, no!" Gloria reared back on the seat. "I love my shister, Neil."

"I'm not Neil, Gloria. I'm Dusty."

"Oh, yeah." She looked at him without recognition. "Okay, so maybe I'm the teeniest little bit jealous of Mimi." She held up one diamond-bedecked hand, finally bringing together her thumb and forefinger until they touched. "She always could'a had any guy she wanted—they just lined up for her. But she's been dumb—you know, cute but poor. Now she's found one who's cute but *rich.*"

*Jesus, what's she saying?* He wanted to ask but was afraid of what the answer might be. Grim-faced and tight-lipped, he drove on.

"After a certain age, cute don't cut it no more," Gloria mumbled.

He didn't want to listen but he couldn't help himself.

"You'd be surprised how easy it is to make love to a man if there's enough cash involved. They'll believe anything, especially in bed." She giggled. "How the hell do you think I got set up? Mimi's no damned better than I am, Neil!" She swayed on the seat, her head swinging in an exaggerated circle. "You're not Neil. Where the hell's Neil?"

"Forget Neil. We were talking about Mimi."

"Everybody's always talking about Mimi." She flounced around on the seat. "She said she'd sheen the light. Well, hell, I drew up a list!" Her tone grew boastful. "I said, 'Okay, girl, here's the richest and most eligible men in town. You take it from there.'" She slumped back, her head bobbing limply. "And she did. Boy, howdy, did she! Could'a had three out of three."

Dusty's stomach lurched and the blood hammered in his ears. *The only thing she loves about me is my money, the same thing my mother loved about Harry Chalmers. Mimi's no better than a whore—no better than Melinda. Worse—Melinda never claimed to love me.*

Gloria leaned toward him and squeezed his thigh. "But you were on the top of the list, Dusty-babe," she crooned. "You were on the *very* top of my list. And look how nice everything's worked out! Hot damn!"

*Damn!*

DUSTY HALF CARRIED GLORIA to the couch in her living room, tipped her onto it and stood there while she tried to rise, failed, and fell asleep, all within the space of three minutes. Then he locked her front door, walked calmly back to his car and tried to put his fist through the side window.

The window cracked and gave but didn't shatter. He felt as if the bones of his right hand did, however, and he welcomed the pain. For an instant it cleansed his mind of all else, took him back to another time and place before he'd ever heard of Mimi Carlton.

Took him back to Melinda. Pain had excited Melinda—his pain, anyway. "Broken bones to a cowboy is like a headache to normal people," she used to brag. The violence of rodeo had appealed mightily to her, as had other forms of violence—fights, preferably over her, and wild lovemaking.

But no more. Melinda was dead, killed in a barroom brawl in Texas more than a year ago. When his attorney had brought him the news, Dusty had felt nothing at all, except maybe pity—pity and regret that the trail to Lori had dead-ended yet again.

Mimi wasn't like Melinda. With Melinda what he'd seen was what he'd got. With Mimi everything was a sham. She'd come to town looking for a meal ticket and she'd found one—or three, if Gloria was to be believed. Why not? Out of the mouths of babes and drunks . . .

In a matter of weeks, Mimi had attained the unattainable—a marriage proposal from a man who'd sworn he'd never tie the knot again. She'd gone unerringly to his weaknesses and he'd managed only a token resistance.

He climbed behind the wheel and sat there for a moment with his head down, concentrating on controlling his pain. After a while he started the engine and drove slowly and carefully down the driveway—because everything in him demanded otherwise.

Driving home he faced the truth.

It wasn't so much Mimi's mercenary nature that enraged him. The truth was, he could forgive her anything except convincing him she loved him.

## 11

DANNY WOKE UP SCREAMING in the dark, something he'd never done before. Mimi, waiting in Dusty's bedroom, hurried into the nursery. Her long white cotton nightgown billowed around her as she lifted the baby into her arms.

"Poor angel," she crooned. Snuggling him against her breast, she swayed back and forth until he quieted. Then she carried him into the big master bedroom and sat down on the window seat overlooking the front of the house. Danny's eyes closed and he sighed.

She oughtn't to have been surprised to find Danny too wound up to sleep. It had been a stressful party for him, too, she supposed. At one point J.D. had called the baby a "party favor," and that was how he must have felt as he was passed from hand to adoring hand.

He didn't know how lucky he was, Mimi thought glumly. At least he hadn't had to deal with Gloria.

*I'll have to say something to her tomorrow about her drinking*, Mimi realized. *I should have brought it up a long time ago, but I knew I'd hurt her feelings*. Now the problem had reached a point where something had to be done, regardless.

She saw the lights of Dusty's car far down the road and her mood brightened. Watching his approach, a small bemused smile curved her lips. She loved Dusty and he loved her—she grew more certain of that all the time. Someday soon he'd realize it, too. In the meantime she'd do everything in her power to earn his trust, for that was the key.

She heard the front door open, then the creak of the stairs beneath his booted feet. Moving carefully to avoid disturbing the sleeping baby, Mimi carried him back to bed. For a moment she stood beside the crib, holding Danny close to her heart. Then she kissed the top of his head and lowered him gently into his bed.

He sighed and flopped onto his belly, pulling his knees up under him. Smiling at his shadowed form, Mimi tucked in his blanket and tiptoed out.

Dusty stood by the window seat, his back toward her. A chill shot down her spine and she shook it off. Moving lightly, she hurried to him and slipped her arms around his waist.

"You were gone so long!" She nuzzled her cheek against the corded muscles of his back. "I missed you."

He turned, forcing her arms wide. He towered above her, an intimidating shadow in the dimly lighted room.

She shivered. "Danny woke up crying. Poor little guy was too tired to sleep, I guess. I just put him back to bed."

Dusty didn't answer. He didn't put his arms around her or respond in any way. He just looked at her, his face expressionless.

She licked dry lips. "Dusty, what's wrong?"

For a minute she thought he would ignore the question. Then he reached for her, twisting one hand in the front of her nightgown. Slowly and deliberately he dragged her up and toward him, until only her toes touched the carpet. Instinctively her hands covered his to relieve the pressure of his grip.

When her face was only inches from his, he spoke in a soft, chilling voice. "What could possibly be wrong?"

She tried to shrink away, but he controlled her easily. With his free hand he grabbed her chin and held her face still. For a long moment he stared at her as if he'd never seen her before . . . and then he kissed her.

He had never touched her in anger. Why he should do so now she could not imagine. As his lips moved aggressively over hers, she felt the first stirrings of panic. His anger frightened her; his strength overwhelmed her.

Yet his very urgency spoke to her on some deep, primitive level. *He needs me more now than ever,* she thought. *Whatever has happened, it's something he can't bear alone.* Besides, he would never hurt her, she was sure of that. Pretty sure, anyway. . . .

She felt like a doll in his arms with no will of her own as he lowered her until her feet were on the floor again. At the same time he maintained the hard pressure on her mouth. Twisting one hand in her hair, he clamped the other at the base of her spine and arched her backward. She bent before him, stunned by the ruthless assault of his mouth and the careless way he handled her.

And so she fought back, in her own way . . . with lips that softened beneath his hard mouth and hands that stroked instead of seized. It seemed hopeless; she thought his response would never come, but at last it did. Slowly, reluctantly, bitterly . . . his kiss changed, grew tender and yearning. Restraint became an embrace.

He lifted his head and she heard his harsh breathing. No longer self-controlled, he shoved her away.

His eyes glittered and he spoke in a stranger's voice. "I thought I could do it."

Mimi's blood ran cold. "Do what, Dusty?"

He used a short Anglo-Saxon verb that staggered her. She couldn't have been more astonished if he'd hit her.

"W-what are you talking about?" she gasped, one hand flying to her throat.

"Hey, you've been doing it to me." He fumbled in his pocket, drew out something—his wallet? She couldn't be sure, was too dazed to care.

He went on in that same harsh, mocking voice. "I thought I was a pretty cool customer, but you make me look like a greenhorn, babe. I guess it really *is* as easy for you to screw a rich man as a poor man—and a damned sight more profitable."

*It's as easy to love a rich man as a poor man*—a bastardized version of Gloria's words. Oh, God, he thought she wanted him for his money! "Dusty, please let me explain...."

He caught hold of her wrist and pressed something against her palm—money, she saw with horror. Falling back before his relentless advance, she felt the edge of the bed against her knees. He released her suddenly and she toppled onto the bedspread.

Paper bills rained down around her.

His tall figure towered over her like some awful apparition. "You're a liar," he said in a curiously disembodied voice. "I hate a liar."

She struggled up on the bed. "Whatever Gloria said—"

"You know what Gloria said."

"I don't! Gloria was drunk—she could have said anything." All those crumpled bills on top of the candlewick bedspread affronted her and she shoved them aside and reached for him.

She caught his hand in hers and he flinched. He looked as if he was in pain—actual physical pain. When she glanced down at his swollen and bruised flesh, she realized he was.

"Dusty, your hand . . ."

He shook her off. "I don't care a hoot in hell about my hand." He flexed it, rubbing at the battered knuckles. His eyes burned into her. "Why'd you do it, Mimi? Why'd you do it to me?"

"Do what? I don't even know what I'm denying!" Sick with dread, she knelt on the bed with her hands clasped before her, the nightgown pooling around her.

"Did you or did you not set out to marry a rich man?"

"No! That was just a . . . a joke. I was sitting in a Denver motel with my son and less than a thousand dollars to my name and I made a birthday wish. It was silly—it never meant anything!"

"No?" His brow curved up in a sardonic line.

"*That's* what you're so mad about? You think I want to marry you for your money? Dusty, if all I wanted was a rich husband, I could have gone after Martin, I could have gone after Max—"

"You did. Maybe they failed their auditions." He jerked his head toward the bed. "Seems unlikely—enough cash makes just about anything all right, according to your sister."

That's when Mimi knew it was hopeless. If he could think her capable of that, knowing her as he did, he could think her capable of anything. "Damn you, Dusty! You want the truth, the whole truth?"

A shadow passed over his face—apprehension? There was no such uncertainty in his voice, however. "That's all I ever wanted."

"Then here it is. I fell in love with you, damn it! I thought I could have it all—love, financial security, a wonderful man who would take care of me and my son. I love you for richer or poorer, and you just happen to be richer. I don't know any way to convince you of—wait a minute!" The answer seemed so obvious. "I'll sign a prenuptial agreement, sight unseen," she decided, thinking out loud.

"Prenuptial, hell!" He grabbed her by both elbows and hauled her up off the bed. "Here's my offer, take it or leave it. You can stay as my mistress. I'll pay you for services rendered but I'll never marry you. Period."

She slapped him. Without considering consequences, she hauled back her right arm and slashed her open palm across his cheek. His head snapped back and the sound of flesh on flesh cracked through the room.

Mimi's mouth rounded in a horrified O and she stared at him in dismay. She had never struck another human being in her life; she hadn't even spanked her son. She didn't believe in corporal punishment. She believed in reason. She believed in the power of love.

He reached up to stroke the dark, angry stain on his cheek. She'd never seen his blue eyes so stormy or his jaw so relentlessly clinched.

"I'm sorry," she gasped. "I can't believe I did that."

"Don't worry," he said. "You'll pay for it." His glance skimmed past her and settled on the bed.

"No!" Her voice trembled. "Not in anger, Dusty."

"What's the difference if the money's good?" He tugged at his shirttail, keeping his eyes on her.

She whirled and flung herself toward the far side of the bed, but he was too quick for her. Throwing himself forward, he caught her by the ankle and hauled her back. She fought him grimly, silently—hopelessly.

He wrestled her onto her back and tumbled on top of her, both her wrists secured above her head in one of his big hands. With his free hand he reached between them for the buttons on her gown.

"Time to pay the piper," he grunted.

A shriek from the baby's room cut between them and they both froze. Dusty's head jerked back and his nostrils flared as he stared toward the closed door.

Mimi felt the lessening of tension in the hands that held her and seized her chance. "Let me go!" she cried. "Danny needs me!"

For a moment she thought he wasn't going to respond, but then he did, rolling away and pushing back and off the bed. Quickly she scooted to the opposite side and stood up. They faced each other across what should have been their marriage bed, but now would never be.

"Danny needs you. I don't." He turned away.

"Dusty. Wait a minute."

He halted halfway to the door. She tugged the diamond engagement ring from her finger and looked up, seeing him through a haze of tears. "Don't forget this," she whispered, holding out the ring.

"Keep it," he said, his voice filled with contempt. "You earned it."

A terrible helplessness settled over her. "No," she said in a strangled voice. "I don't want it. All I ever wanted was you." She swallowed hard. "J.D. and I—we'll leave tomorrow. I'll take nothing with me except what I brought. You won't need to count the silverware or inventory the antiques."

*That's a damned lie,* Dusty thought, even as he shrugged and walked out of the room. When she left tomorrow, she'd take his last chance of happiness.

DUSTY DROVE AROUND most of the night, ending up in a twenty-four-hour diner in San Diego. Brooding over a cup of bad coffee at 5:00 a.m., he edged closer to the decision he'd been wrestling with for weeks.

He had never been loved—not by mother, wife or daughter. Over the years he had concluded that somehow he wasn't worthy of love. Eventually he'd grown accustomed to being alone, and he could do it again. He knew he could.

Only now he didn't want to. Not after the joy he'd found with Mimi and J.D. and Danny.

His mother had married for money; Melinda had left him for more money; Mimi had wanted him because now he had money. Lori? She was pulling some scam with dollar signs attached, as sure as the Lord made little green apples.

But Mimi had fooled him worst of all. He almost wished he hadn't found out about her cupidity, although that was cowardly. He had, and now she'd leave and take J.D. with her.

That left Danny.

Dusty dropped bills onto the counter and walked outside to a public telephone at one corner of the restaurant. From memory he dialed his attorney's home telephone number.

After a dozen rings, a groggy voice came onto the line. "Yeah?"

"Dusty McLain. I need to see you, Tom. Be at my place at eleven."

"Damn—what time is it? Son of a—it's Sunday!"

"Just be there."

"What the hell's going on?" The fretful edge left the attorney's voice, replaced by cautious alarm.

Dusty hesitated. "It's that personal matter I mentioned to you a few weeks ago."

"Custody? Damn, Dusty, I thought you'd decided—"

Dusty hung up.

MIMI OFFERED DANNY another bite of cereal and the baby lunged at it, knocking the spoon out of her hand.

She looked down blankly at the sticky white goop on the kitchen floor. Sighing, she handed the baby a teething biscuit and bent to clean up the mess with a paper towel.

She straightened and he offered her a grin, to which she didn't respond. She didn't feel like smiling this morning, not even at Danny. She had barely survived a night of tears and self-recrimination and was so tired and miserable that it didn't seem humanly possible to get through what this day threatened to become.

The house was a shambles in the aftermath of the party. Maria would be in soon to help clean up and that would mean explanations Mimi wasn't eager to make.

Morrissy and J.D. had prepared their own breakfast by the time Mimi had straggled downstairs with Danny in her arms. They'd taken one look at her and beaten a hasty retreat.

She heard the front door open and panic leaped in her breast. Dusty was back. Where he'd been or what he'd been doing, she couldn't imagine. She only knew she couldn't face him. Not yet. Maybe never.

She heard his footsteps on the stairs and relaxed a little. Perhaps he'd found a new nanny. The possibility alarmed her, even as she admitted it would be best.

The back door banged open and J.D. scooted inside. "Was that Dusty?" he inquired. "I gotta talk to him."

"J.D., wait!"

The boy skidded to a stop, giving his mother a curious glance. "You don't look so good this morning, Mom. Too much celebrating?" He grinned.

Looking at him, Mimi felt sick. What she had to tell him was going to bring his world to an end as surely as it had hers. Thank God, he was so mature for his age. She could make him understand.

She had to. She motioned to an empty chair. "I need to talk to you, hon."

He glanced at the hall door, then at the chair. "Ahh . . . can it wait?"

"I'm afraid not. This is important."

"Okay." He returned to the table and slumped into the chair, sticking out his skinny, blue-jeaned legs. As always these days he wore boots. He gave her a surprisingly compassionate look, as if he sensed her difficulty. "Did I tell you Dusty said I could call him Dad after you two get married?" he asked.

Mimi's heart clenched into a knot of misery. "J.D., about that . . ." She tried to conceal her anguish.

"You don't want me to?" The boy frowned. "I didn't think it was disloyal to Dad, but if you do . . . I mean, he knows—he knew I loved him." He reached out awkwardly to pat her hand, his earnest face baffled. "Don't cry, Mom."

She hadn't known until then that she was weeping. She brushed at her damp cheeks. "J.D., it's off," she blurted. "The engagement's off. We'll be moving out today." *But not back to Gloria's—anywhere but there!*

He recoiled, going pale beneath the freckles. His mouth worked, but no sound came out.

"It's nobody's fault," Mimi rushed on, trying to give him a chance to recover. "We made a mistake, that's all. I know you're disappointed—I am, too, but—"

"*No!*" J.D. bolted to his feet, his narrow shoulders hunched and his eyes wild. "You can't do this to me! I won't let you!"

"J.D.!" Dismayed, Mimi stared at her son.

Danny seemed equally shocked. He frowned and thrust out his lower lip, his eyes squeezed shut and he let out a bloodcurdling scream.

"I love Dusty!" J.D. yelled over the noise of the baby. "And Mr. Swain and I—jeez, I even kinda like the brat!"

Mimi stood up and tried to put her arms around her trembling son. "I love all of them, too, baby, but—"

"I'm not your baby!" J.D. shrugged her off and backed away, his expression accusing her. "This is all your fault!"

She flinched at his denunciation. "That's not true," she faltered. "Something happened—he misunderstood."

"He's crazy about you! Everybody says so. Please, Mom, tell him you've changed your mind," J.D. pleaded. "Tell him you'll marry him."

His desperation pierced her, but she dared not give him hope where none existed. "I'm not the one who broke it off," she said. "He did."

For a moment it didn't look as if he believed her. Then his face grew hard, too hard for his years. "What did you do, Mom?" he yelled at her. "It must have been really awful!" He turned and bolted for the door.

"J.D.! Wait!"

She started after him, just as Danny let loose with a new round of complaints. She didn't dare leave him alone in the high chair. She yanked aside the tray and snatched him up—only he didn't come. Securely belted in place, he uttered a soft, indignant grunt and gazed at her with incensed blue eyes.

By the time she got Danny unhooked, into her arms and both of them down the hall, the front door was closing. Running out onto the front steps into early-morning drizzle, she stopped and cast about wildly for J.D. He was nowhere to be seen.

But something else was—Neil Gordon's Ford, pulling slowly into the driveway. For a minute Mimi debated the wisdom of facing her sister under the circumstances and finally decided it couldn't be put off.

Besides, she'd spent untold miserable hours last night rehearsing what she'd say, beginning with *"How could you do this to me, your own sister?"* And so she waited at the top of the steps beneath the porch overhang, her face stiff and unwelcoming.

Neil got out and walked around to assist Gloria. She climbed out of the car and clung to the door for a moment. She wore oversize dark glasses, despite the fact that the day was dark and gloomy; even from this distance Mimi could see Gloria had the shakes.

Neil said something and Gloria nodded. Taking a deep breath she closed the car door. She moved toward the porch as if walking barefoot on glass shards, picking up her feet and putting them down with enormous effort. At the steps she looked up at Mimi.

"Where's Dusty?" she croaked. "I think I owe my future brother-in-law an apology."

"He's not your future brother-in-law anymore, and if you owe anybody an apology..."

Gloria's face crumpled. Mimi bit off her hot words, acutely aware that she was about to say things that would stand between them forever. Looking down at her sister, she felt the anger begin to lose its power over her. Gloria had made a mistake, but not out of malice; Mimi would never believe it was malicious.

Nor had Dusty acted maliciously. He'd been hurt and had lashed out, but he would suffer more than anyone else for his lack of faith. Yes, even more than Mimi; although she might never fill the empty space he'd left in her heart, still she had people who loved her and whom she loved in return. Dusty had no one. No one except a baby whose mother would claim him soon.

And so Mimi looked at Gloria, at the tears gathering in her eyes, and finished more gently. "If you owe anybody an apology, Gloria, I think it's you. How long are you going to keep doing this to yourself? Honey, you need help!"

DUSTY LOOKED OUT of the big curved window of his second-story bedroom just as Neil and Gloria drove up. *Returning to the scene of the crime,* he thought bitterly. He couldn't hear what was said, but he saw Gloria sit down on the bottom step, put her arms upon her knees and her head upon her arms, and heard her utter an agonized "Aargh!"

He could imagine what Mimi must have said. Well, she wasn't going to get away with putting all the blame on Gloria. He'd set the record straight in a hurry!

He took the stairs two at a time, just itching for a fight. Crossing the wide hall in a couple of galloping strides, he threw open the door. Mimi knelt in front of her sister, holding both of Gloria's hands and talking earnestly. Neil stood in the shelter of the porch, an arm looped around Danny's middle.

At Dusty's unceremonious arrival Mimi glanced up. She looked exhausted, dark smudges beneath her eyes and lines of strain around her mouth. She started to speak, but Gloria touched her arm almost beseechingly. "Go take care of the baby, girl, and let me talk to Dusty."

"Are you sure?" Mimi glanced back at Danny, wiggling around in Neil's arms.

"She's sure." Neil waited for Mimi to rise and then thrust the baby into her arms. "Don't worry. I'll stay right here."

The look he gave Dusty was clearly challenging. Apparently Neil was content not to interfere between the sisters, but felt a sufficiently proprietary interest in Gloria not to leave her alone with a man who had reason to wish her ill.

Mimi's unhappy gaze passed between Dusty and Gloria. Seeing no encouragement to stay from either, the starch seemed to go out of her. "This is really hard," she whispered, "especially considering that I love you both."

Holding Danny in her arms, she walked back inside the house with all the dignity in the world.

*Why would she say that now?* Dusty wondered irritably. After everything that had happened, did she think him foolish enough to believe it? Maybe she was just trying to give the knife one more twist.

Gloria stood slowly. She seemed to have aged twenty years in the last twenty-four hours. "You look like I feel— *real* bad." She said it as if that likelihood gave her considerable pleasure.

"And I came down here to defend you." He gave her a sour look. "You here to finish me off?"

"I came to apologize. I came to throw myself on your mercy. Don't think that's easy with the granddaddy of all hangovers."

"Gloria," he said, going against the nonintervention policy that had served him for a lifetime, "as a friend, I've got to tell you that you drink too much."

She didn't flinch. "Yeah, I know. Neil and Mimi already mentioned that." She gave Neil a quick, grateful glance. "Monday I'm going to ask my doc to check me into the Betty Ford Clinic. If I have to suffer, it may as well be in fashionable surroundings."

"Fair enough." Dusty didn't like feeling so relieved to hear this. He didn't want to care.

She eyed him askance. "Now it's my turn. You, my friend, are an unmitigated asshole."

Neil gave Dusty a quick glance that said *I agree* and took Gloria's arm. The three moved slowly toward the car.

"Care to elaborate, or am I just your everyday garden-variety asshole?" Dusty inquired. He'd been called worse; hell, he'd called *himself* worse.

Recently, as a matter of fact.

She stopped and turned to face him, and for a moment she was the old Gloria. Her survey began at his hairline, flicked down over his face, his chest, his legs, all the way to his feet and up again. She smiled. "There's nothing garden-variety about you in any way. When you're smart you're very smart, and when you're dumb you're an asshole. Where my sister is concerned, you've been exceedingly dumb."

He refused to rise to the bait. "Can't argue with that."

She took off her dark glasses and peered at him through bloodshot eyes. "Shut up and listen. I may get sick any minute and forget what I'm trying to tell you."

"Which is?"

"That you should have considered the source." She sounded completely disgusted. "Did it ever occur to you that although I love my sister, I might be jealous of her? Think about it—she's been married once, to her childhood sweetheart, a man she loved. She went through hell with him while he was sick . . . and then he died."

She shook her head and sighed. "I, on the other hand, have been married three times to wealthy men, two of whom I could actually stand being in the same room with after the first month. Of course I urged my destitute sister to go after a wealthy man—it's a conditioned response. Of course I refused to believe her when she said she was falling in love with you—and she did say it."

Neil opened her car door and she plopped herself inside. "Of course I was jealous when it looked like she was going to walk away with love *and* money. Hell, I'm no saint, but I thought I could control my baser instincts. And I did . . . for a while."

She closed the car door and rolled down the window as Neil walked around to the driver's side. "Let me tell you something about my sister. You've treated her like dirt, but is she out to get even? No—she's worried about what's going to happen to you when she's gone. She's worried about Danny and about J.D., and even about Morrissy and Maria. If I was her . . . if I was her and she was me, I'd kill her and then I'd kill you. And what does she do? She says she loves us."

She leaned back in her seat and closed her eyes. Neil started the car and they drove away, leaving Dusty standing there knee-deep in doubt. After the car was completely out of sight, he turned and walked slowly back into the house.

Maria was polishing furniture when he entered the library. She looked up, a can of spray wax in one hand and a soft cloth in the other.

"I've got work to do in here," he said. "If you could speed things up I'd appreci—"

Maria's eyes flashed and a torrent of Spanish gushed forth. She threw down her polishing cloth with a flourish, still talking a blue streak. He caught very little of what she was saying—something about Mimi, something about a fool—but it was easy enough to guess that he was the target of her tirade. Bursting into tears, she ran from the room.

Jesus! The entire female population of the free world seemed to have it in for him today. He really *didn't* understand women.

MORRISSY STOMPED into the library shortly before eleven with a burr under his saddle. Dusty looked up from the pile of paperwork, relieved to see it wasn't a female. He'd had about all of them he could take.

His relief was short-lived.

Morrissy put his fists on the desk and leaned forward with slitted eyes. "The boy's out in the barn cryin' his eyes out, the little maverick's caterwaulin' in that baby cage a' his, Mimi's upstairs packin' and a-snivelin', and that Maria's talkin' Mex to herself and throwin' dirty laundry all over the back porch."

Dusty grimaced. "So?"

"*So what you gonna do about it?*"

Dusty slumped back in his chair. "*Et tu, Brute?*"

"I don't know nothin' about no Bru-tay, but the rest a' the herd's plenty riled up, I can tell you. You're the big bull in this pasture, so it's dang well up to you to do somethin'. Marry that little gal and put ever'body outta their misery—includin' you."

Morrissy was not one to give advice except in general philosophical terms. That he did so now astonished Dusty, but changed nothing. "Can't do that, Morrissy."

The little man reared back. "Thought you give your word."

"I did." Dusty hesitated; he couldn't say this to anyone but Morrissy. "And then I found out she's no different than any other woman I ever knew. She's after the bucks."

Morrissy snorted disparagingly. "I wouldn't believe that if'n she said it to my face. Neither would you, if you had the sense God give a goose." He spun around and stomped out of the room.

Dusty was still stinging from Morrissy's tongue-lashing when he heard the pounding of the door knocker promptly at eleven o'clock. Tom was on time, Dusty thought, waiting for someone to let the attorney in.

No one did. Tom knocked again, louder. Dusty waited. Nothing. Swearing, he walked into the hall and threw open the door.

His longtime attorney stood on the porch with a puzzled expression on his round face. Instead of his usual dark suit and conservative tie, he wore casual clothing and a Windbreaker beaded with mist. "Where is everybody?" he asked, following Dusty into the library.

"Who knows? Around someplace." Dusty waved vaguely and pulled out the chair behind the antique Victorian desk. "Mimi and I called it quits last night and everybody's taking sides." *Yeah, sides against me.* "It's a damned mess."

"Sorry to hear that." Tom put his briefcase upon the desk. "She seemed like quite a lovely girl, exactly what you need—"

"I need legal advice." Dusty gestured to the chair in front of the desk. The more everybody pushed, the more his resolve hardened. "My personal life is my business."

"Personal life! Ha!" Tom sat down. "Until recently, your personal life consisted of occasional and inappropriate liaisons heading nowhere. Dangerous, with your assets. You're damned lucky someone hasn't hauled your assets into palimony court already." Tom chuckled at his own wit.

"Not lucky, careful." Dusty picked up a glass paperweight and hefted it as if ready to heave it at the jocular attorney. "Which is why I want to know how to go about gaining custody of my grandson. It should be easy, since his mother's abandoned him."

Instantly Tom sobered. "You can't be sure," he said, assuming his attorney persona. "I keep trying to tell you, the situation's not that cut-and-dried." He hesitated. "Why are you pushing this now?"

"Because it's in the best interests of the child."

"You love him, then." Dusty saw Tom watching closely for any reaction.

"I . . ." *Say it*, Dusty raged at himself. *It's true—why can't you say it?* "He's my grandson."

Tom grunted reproachfully. "I would advise you, both as your lawyer and your friend, to think twice before you do something irrevocable," he said. "We've still got investigators looking for your daughter and we'll find her in time—either that or she'll come back. If you antagonize her and lose . . . Well, I shouldn't have to point out that you could be left with exactly nothing, neither daughter nor grandson."

Dusty kept his face impassive, although Tom's warning struck deep at his insecurities. But he was committed; he couldn't back off now. "You shouldn't have to point that out, but you did," he said. "You've done your duty. Can we get on with it? What do we do first?"

Tom looked as if he'd like to argue the point further. Instead he shrugged. "Fine. Just so you're sure. Now, the first thing we—"

The clang of the door knocker intruded for what seemed the tenth time that morning. Dusty glanced toward the sound with unconcealed impatience. "Let Mimi or J.D. get it. You were saying?"

"That Monday morning you'll need to come to my office so we can—"

Another flurry of knocking; Dusty frowned. "Where the hell is everybody today, on strike?" He rose. "This place has been worse than Grand Central Station."

He stalked to the front door. Through the stained-glass panes he could see two shadowy figures on the front step, one considerably taller than the other. Who the hell? he wondered, flinging open the door.

A man and a woman stood there, or maybe a boy and a girl, for they were young, early twenties or even late teens. They were holding hands. They faced the opening door almost defensively, it seemed to Dusty, as if they didn't know what would appear on the other side.

"Yes?" he said brusquely.

The girl took an uncertain step forward, her free hand fluttering up. Her blue eyes brimmed with tears and her smile faltered.

"Daddy," she whispered, "it's me, Lori. I . . . I've come back for my baby."

# 12

LORI TOOK A JERKY STEP toward her father. She stopped short and glanced over her shoulder at the young man, who gave her a quick nod. That was all the encouragement she needed. She hurled herself against Dusty's chest and clung to him, trembling.

Dusty stood there paralyzed, incapable of responding to this stranger's appeal. His arms, his legs, his very mind were powerless. *She looks so like Melinda*, he thought, *except for the blue eyes*. But her coltish grace was all her own, and he'd seen a sweetness in her face that had never been her mother's.

Lori pulled back, dashing at tear-streaked cheeks with the back of one hand. "I'm sorry," she said, almost choking. "It's just—I was beginning to think this day would never come." She took a deep breath and looked around hopefully. "Where's Danny? Where's my baby?"

The young man slipped an arm around her shoulders. "Slow down, honey," he said in a surprisingly deep voice. "Give your old man time to catch his breath." He thrust out one hand. "I'm Kevin Kelly."

Dusty looked down blankly at the proffered hand, then at the boy's face. He made no move to shake hands.

Kevin looked disconcerted; then understanding seemed to hit him and he grinned. "I'm Danny's father," he said, as guilelessly as if that were sure to be recommendation enough.

Dusty stared at the two kids and something inside him shriveled up and died. They were typical of their time and place: sun-bleached hair too long; smooth, tanned skin; frayed and faded T-shirts advocating Save the Whales; patched and ragged jeans. But that wasn't all he saw.

He saw love. He saw love in Kevin's protectiveness toward Lori, and in the way she turned her big blue eyes toward him for support—big blue eyes so like Danny's.

*Blue eyes so like mine, according to Mimi.* With an effort, Dusty shook off his shock and spoke the first words he'd said to his daughter face-to-face in almost three years.

"What the hell are you doing here *now?*"

MIMI HOVERED in the shadows at the top of the stairs. She ached to be at Dusty's side, but she no longer had that right. Still, she felt his pain.

"Come into the library so we can talk," Dusty was saying in a raspy voice. As he turned she saw his face, filled with helpless grief.

He led the way and the two kids followed obediently. Their expressions reflected their awe as they looked around the entry hall. Lori must have known her father was wealthy, but the full impact of what that meant appeared to be only just sinking in. It put her at an even greater disadvantage.

Mimi stood perfectly still until the three disappeared. For a moment longer she hesitated, knowing she should turn around and leave. But she couldn't—she *had* to know what was going on in there. She hurried to the partially open door and positioned herself so she could eavesdrop without being seen.

Dusty was introducing Tom Attridge.

"A lawyer?" Lori sounded alarmed.

Dusty squared his shoulders almost imperceptibly. He appeared perfectly calm. "You can't abandon your baby and then waltz back in here anytime it's convenient and take him back," he said with no more feeling than if he'd been discussing the abandonment of a puppy. "That's no way to raise a kid." He turned, just enough so he wasn't looking directly at Lori. "So I've decided to keep him."

Panic flared in the girl's eyes. "I love my baby!" she exclaimed shrilly. She appealed to Kevin, "What's he talking about? Can they do this?"

"No way!" Kevin glowered at the two older men. "You mess with us and we'll take the kid someplace where you'll never find him!"

It was the wrong thing to say to Dusty. He came around with hands clenching into fists, all his self-control gone in a flash. His scorn included Lori. "Like mother, like daughter. This time I'm taking no chances. I'm going for legal custody and I'll get it. You don't love that baby—hell, you dumped him. He's better off with me."

"That's not true! There were...reasons." Her tears fell in earnest. Watching through the crack in the door, Mimi dug her fingernails into her palms, unable to look away.

"I'll just bet there were reasons." Dusty's lip curled. "Was the surf up?"

Lori recoiled and uttered a little gasp of outrage. Kevin put his arms around her until she got hold of herself again.

"I'll tell 'em," he said grimly. He straightened and glared at Dusty. "Let's get a few things straight. You're looking at us like we're trash and that's not fair."

"I'm sure he didn't mean—" Tom jumped in, but Dusty cut him off.

"You two married or just living together?" His inference was clear: only trash cohabited.

Trash and rich guys who were afraid of marriage. Mimi gritted her teeth.

Kevin's jaw jutted out. "We're married! And we're responsible citizens. I'm a student at State and both of us hold down jobs. It's not easy, but once I graduate..." His eyes glittered with determination. "I admit we don't exactly live in La Jolla, but we're making it." He hesitated. "Or at least, we were until—"

"Until what?" Tom's curiosity appeared to get the better of him.

"Lori was a witness in a drug trial in San Diego. Some really bad dudes were looking for us and—"

"Drugs!" Dusty looked as if his worst fears had been confirmed. He glanced at his lawyer, but his face betrayed more grief than reproach.

"Hold it, man!" Kevin stepped forward, an angry flush rising in his cheeks. "We're not into drugs, if that's what you're thinking. A bad drug deal went down behind the restaurant where Lori worked, and she accidentally got a good look at some of the guys involved."

Dusty made a scornful sound. "The cops protect witnesses."

"The cops *try* to protect witnesses."

Kevin reached for the hem of his T-shirt and flipped it up, turning to face Dusty. Dusty's eyes widened, then narrowed into angry slits.

Kevin dragged his shirt back down. "We were ambushed," he continued matter-of-factly. "We'd just come out of a grocery store. They fired a half-dozen shots. We were damned lucky."

Lori clutched Kevin's arm. "I was holding Danny. Kevin jumped in front of us. If he hadn't..."

She shivered, and so did Mimi.

Kevin looked uncomfortable with all the attention. "Yeah, well, the cops said they'd beef up our protection after that." He shrugged. "Then Lori got the bright idea of leaving Danny with his grandfather for safekeeping."

The downward curve of Kevin's mouth conveyed his opinion of how well that had worked out.

Lori's face looked haunted. "I didn't know what else to do, Daddy. With Mama gone—did you know about that?"

"Not until I started looking for you."

The girl nodded. "Almost two years ago. I wanted to tell you but . . ."

Her voice trailed away. Mimi finished the thought. *But you're a stranger. I wasn't sure you'd care.*

Lori and Dusty faced each other. Mimi, seeing them in profile, felt the tension streaking between them. She had never seen Dusty look quite so near the edge of control, and his daughter seemed in an equally fragile emotional state. Mimi held her breath and said a silent prayer for them both.

Lori licked her lips, but her concentration on her father didn't waver. "I know you never loved me," she said in a brave little voice that refused to sink into self-pity. "I always knew that, even without Mama always—" She stopped short, chewing on her bottom lip.

Dusty's face was a mask, but Mimi saw below that cold surface. Lori's words cut him to the quick; he was bleeding, but he wouldn't let it show. *If only he would,* she thought. *If only he'd acknowledge his humanity.*

But he wouldn't, not unless . . . Mimi pressed her fingers to her mouth. Not unless something forced his hand, and she knew what that something might be.

INSIDE THE LIBRARY, Dusty stared at his daughter. Once, after a particularly nasty spill in a rodeo arena, he'd gone into shock. That's was how he felt now—as blank and vacant as if he stood apart and watched some other poor son of a bitch bleeding to death.

Lori was still talking. "... but then I remembered the necklace." She bit her lip and dropped her gaze. "I knew you were mad about that, but I didn't think you'd take it out on an innocent baby. I was afraid to ask you to take Danny, though. What if I brought him to you and you told me to forget it? What could I have done then?"

Her head slumped, her long, sun-bleached hair swinging forward to shield her expression. "I couldn't take that chance," she whispered, "so I just left him in your truck and prayed."

He ached for her, but bitter experience held him hostage. The last time he'd tried to touch her—put his arms around her—had been when he'd given her that necklace. She'd thrown it into his face and screamed at him, *You're mean and selfish and I never want to see you again!*

Now she was singing a different tune and it was beyond his comprehension. Which was the truth? Either? Neither? He cast a half-wild glance at Tom, who looked away.

"I want my baby, Daddy. I want him *now*."

"Hold your horses." Dusty's voice was harsh. "I've got to think."

"Dusty, give her the baby." Tom used his lawyer voice. "Under the circumstances, you don't have a prayer of getting custody." He nodded at the young couple. "You've been talking about the Rival Gangs drug trial that's been going on in San Diego, right?"

"Yeah." Kevin glanced at Lori. "She was an innocent bystander but she—*we*—felt she had to do her duty as a good citizen."

"By going to the police, at considerable risk." Tom appealed to Dusty. "Man, don't fault her for it. The good guys won this one—they got a conviction, thanks mostly to her testimony. Your daughter's a heroine! I've got a friend who worked on that case and he said . . ."

As Tom talked, Dusty felt the numbness replaced by a despair that was worse. He understood what Lori had done, because he would have done the same thing himself. Whatever the cost, he always tried to do what was right. But sometimes it was impossible to know what was right. Like now.

Whichever path he chose, he would lose. Everything was slipping through his fingers. He had driven away his daughter just as he'd driven away Mimi.

Danny would grow up, never knowing his grandfather cared, as his mother had never known her father cared. Mimi would leave, never knowing . . .

Things had gone too far, too fast. Nothing could retrieve the situation—unless he could keep Danny. He'd give the baby everything, including the love he'd kept bottled up for a lifetime. He'd fight for Danny; he'd fight with everything he had.

They were staring at him, waiting for him to say something. A muscle in his jaw jumped; he wanted them out of here, all of them.

He started to say so just as the door opened. Mimi stood there, her expression closed. In her arms she carried a warm and sleepy baby boy, who yawned and smiled at the room in general.

Dusty stared, too shocked to speak. What was Mimi thinking of? Once Kevin and Lori got their hands on that baby it was all over.

And then the realization hit him: *This is how she gets even. She knew how much that baby meant to me, even before I did. She's taking her revenge.* A terrible helplessness settled over him.

Mimi searched Dusty's face, praying for even a glimmer of understanding. She saw none; he thought she had betrayed him and it was no more than he'd expected. His sharp look of anguish would haunt her until the day she died.

But she must do what she'd come to do. *Forgive me, Dusty,* she begged silently. She carried Danny to his mother, holding him out like a peace offering. Lori reached for her baby, joy suffusing her face.

Kevin smiled and leaned down to ruffle the baby's hair. "Hi, there, Tiger. You've grown!"

Lori's gaze met Mimi's. "Thank you," she whispered. "I don't know who you are, but—" her eyes widened "—wait a minute, aren't you—?"

"And you're—!"

The two women stared at each other.

"What?" Kevin asked.

Lori gave him a quick glance. "Remember I told you some woman almost caught me in the parking lot of the feed store? It was her! I hung around until she opened the door to Daddy's truck and then I got out of there."

"I remember," Mimi agreed. "I thought you were just some kid following your father. I'm Mimi Carlton. I tried to take as good care of Danny as you did, Lori."

"He looks wonderful." Lori looked at the baby in her arms for confirmation, her eyes filled with pride. "Thank you."

"Don't thank me, thank his grandfather." Mimi couldn't look at Dusty. Instead she curved her hand around Danny's soft cheek in a gesture of parting. In all likelihood she'd never see the little guy again, and she'd grown to love him as if he were her own flesh and blood.

"Try to understand." She was pleading with Lori now, pleading for a man who stared at her with horrified disbelief. "Your father loves this baby and he loves you, but he doesn't trust you enough to admit it. Why should he, after the hell your mother put him through? I know I shouldn't say that, but *he* won't tell you. If you'll take the time to get to know him . . ."

Understanding lighted Lori's face. "Are you and Daddy . . . ?"

"No." It hurt to say the word but Mimi managed. "Not anymore. But that doesn't change the kind of person he is. There won't be a custody fight, Lori. He'll do the right thing eventually, no matter what it costs him."

"Mimi!"

Dusty's harsh tone sent chills down her spine. He didn't want her interference, but she'd do that and more to save him from himself.

What she couldn't do was look at him. Without another word she turned and walked out of the room. She had done her best. Now his fate, the fate of Lori and Danny, was in other hands.

Dusty started after her, but Lori caught his arm. He looked down at his daughter and grandson, then at the empty doorway, and something inside him snapped.

"I want to understand, Daddy." Lori's voice was tight. "There's so much I want to ask you, so much about you and Mama and me that doesn't make sense." She drew in a quick, shallow breath. "I do know one thing, though. I want us to be a family. Mama . . . Mama said if

I ever came to you, you'd think I was after something—money or something. I'm not."

He wanted to believe; he wanted to tell her so, but his throat closed up and the words wouldn't come. For a long, tense time she looked into his eyes and then she sighed.

"I'm sorry, Daddy," she said. "I thank you from the bottom of my heart for taking care of my baby. That makes up for . . . everything else. I owe you a lot, and if there's ever anything I can do for you . . ."

Anything she could do for him? She could stay here with her husband and child and get to know her father. She could give that father a chance to make up for all the lost years. She could let him try to win her love.

But old habits died hard, and he couldn't say any of those things. He saw her glance at Kevin. She looked exhausted.

Kevin put an arm around her shoulders. "Goodbye, Daddy," she said. "I won't bother you anymore. I just wanted you to know that I . . . love you." She took a step toward the door.

"Wait!"

At Dusty's sharp command, Lori stopped and looked up at him, a question in her eyes. Danny struggled around in his mother's arms and reached out to curl his pudgy fingers into the fabric of his grandfather's shirt. He gave a gentle tug and grinned his innocent baby grin.

Dusty reached for the baby. Alarm flared on Lori's face and her arms tightened protectively. Her glance met her father's, met and held. He hoped she could see what he was feeling, because he didn't know if he could put it into words.

Suddenly her grip on the boy relaxed. Dusty lifted the child and kissed his chubby cheek, feeling a rush of emotion that made him tremble. Lori watched, tears spilling over. Dusty drew her into the closed family circle and kissed the top of her head.

He had trouble making his voice behave. "Mimi was right." It took a great effort to force out the words. "About everything."

Tom turned away as if to respect their privacy. Kevin gaped at the trio, then cleared his throat and followed Tom out of the room.

Dusty tightened his arms around his daughter and grandson. "Lori," he began.

"You don't have to say anything," she offered quickly. "I understand, Daddy."

He felt a surge of relief, then laughed aloud at his own cowardice. "I want to say it." His voice was rough.

Danny blinked in surprise. Dusty felt as if his heart would burst with feelings he'd denied for so long. He was giddy with relief, almost light-headed. "I love you, kid," he told the baby. "I love you, too, Lori."

It was true, and no amount of future hurt would make him regret saying so.

MIMI LEANED against the top pole of the corral, clinging to the rough wood with all her strength. The light rain had stopped, but had left a gray and forlorn day behind.

She would miss this place. She had been happy here, but that was over now. Would anyone ever be happy here again?

The answer to that question depended upon what was happening at this very moment inside the house. If Dusty and Lori could talk, really talk, everything would be all right—Mimi was sure of it. She prayed she'd done the right thing in trying to bring that about; otherwise she'd simply validated Dusty's low opinion of her.

She heard shuffling footsteps behind her and recognized Morrissy's shambling gait. She didn't move.

"You all right, little lady?"

"No," she said. "No, I'm not all right." She lifted her head. "Do you know where J.D. is?"

"Inside that gazebo thing." Morrissy lifted one booted foot onto the bottom rail. He didn't look at her, seemingly more interested in the two horses lazing on the far side of the corral. "Boy's upset."

She gave him a swift glance. "He's not the only one."

"Reckon so." He took his time. "You gonna give Dusty a chance to make all this right?"

"He doesn't know anything needs to *be* made right."

"He will, once he starts thinkin' again." Morrissy spoke with conviction. "Dusty's a good man, but he ain't perfect. He got kicked around a lot as a young'n, mostly by wimmin. If ever a man needed the love of a good woman, it's Dustin McLain."

"We all need love, Morrissy, but most of us don't expect to get it unless we're prepared to give it." She shoved herself away from the corral. "If I don't see you again, I want you to know how much I appreciate all you've done for J.D."

She didn't wait for his response, just hurried away. She tried not to hear the old cowboy's soft, regretful sigh.

SHE FOUND J.D. out behind the gazebo, hunkered down behind it. He held a lariat loosely in his hands, but he didn't look as if he'd been practicing his roping—more likely he just needed something to keep his hands occupied while he did some serious thinking.

"J.D.," she began, "please don't run away again."

He looked up at her with eyes aged by misery. "I'm sorry about that," he said. "Morrissy told me I shouldn't a' acted like a kid."

She sat down on the damp grass, close but not too close. "You didn't let me explain."

He shrugged. "What's to explain, Mom? If it's off, it's off. Nothin' I can do about it." He bit his lip and looked away. "I would a' liked havin' Dusty for my dad, though."

Mimi's throat tightened and for a long time she couldn't answer. When she could, she said softly, "I know how you feel. I would have liked having him for a husband. I guess it just wasn't meant to be."

The boy swung his head toward her, his expression fierce. "Why not?" he cried. "What happened, Mom?"

"He heard . . . something about me."

"A lie?"

"No. The truth. He just . . . put the wrong spin on it."

His brown eyes narrowed. "Like what?"

"You remember my birthday in the motel in Denver, just before we came here?"

"Sure." He frowned. "So what? You lie about your age?"

That earned him a wry smile. "No. When I blew out my candle, I made a birthday wish—to marry a rich man. I'd have been better off if I'd just wished for what I really wanted—Mel Gibson. At least that wouldn't have come back to haunt me."

"He's married, Mom. I heard it on a talk show."

She threw up her hands. "See? I can't even wish right when I get a second chance. My point is, Dusty got it into his head that I wanted to marry *him* for his money."

"So?"

She glanced at her son in surprise. "So it made him mad."

"So was that the reason you wanted to marry him?"

"No! Although . . . in all honesty, it didn't hurt any."

"Did he want to marry you because you're pretty?"

"Certainly not!" Her eyes widened. "You think I'm pretty?"

He grunted in disgust. "You know you're pretty. Beautiful, maybe."

She frowned. "You think that's why he proposed?"

"No, but I don't think it hurt any. At least it makes as much sense as the other." He twisted the rope between his fingers. "Do you guys . . . you know, love each other?"

Mimi sat for a long time, wondering how best to answer that simple, innocent question. He deserved the truth, she decided. "I loved him," she said. "I thought he loved me, although he never said so. Now I realize I was kidding myself, because I wanted us all to live happily ever after. So the answer is yes and no—yes, I loved him, and no, he never loved me."

She looked up to find J.D.'s wide-eyed gaze fixed on some point past her shoulder. Her heart lurched and began to gallop. Without turning, she knew Dusty stood behind her.

"That's not true." Dusty's voice sent shivers up her spine. "It hasn't been true for a long time."

He walked around and squatted on his heels in front of her, his bent knees close but not quite touching her. He looked at her but spoke to J.D.

"I have every intention of marrying your mother, if she'll have me." His glance swung to Mimi. "Will you have me?"

She clenched her hands into fists to keep from grabbing him. "You know what I want to hear," she said in a voice that cracked. *Please, please say it now, Dusty.*

He smiled, a gentle, sensuous smile that eased the strain so vivid on his face. "I love you," he said in a low, experimental tone, and then more loudly, "I love you," and at last fairly shouting, "I love you, damn it! I never believed it was possible to feel this way about anybody." Naked emotion flashed like lightning across his face. "And you love me. At least you used to."

"She still does!" J.D. cried. He added anxiously, "Don't you, Mom?"

Her nod was jerky, but it was all she could manage. She saw the hard tremor pass through Dusty's long body and realized he'd been holding his breath, waiting for her response. It had cost him a lot to expose his deepest emotions and risk rejection.

What he hadn't known until this moment was that it was no risk at all.

Dusty patted J.D.'s shoulder. "Danny's mother is inside," he said gruffly. "Go say hello to your stepsister, son."

A grin split J.D.'s face and he jumped to his feet. "Oh, boy!" he said. "Oh-boy-oh-boy! This makes me the little twerp's uncle! I'll get to boss him around! I'll get to put him down all the time! He'll have to call me 'sir'! I'll get to—"

Dusty watched the boy lope toward the house. Then he went down on his knees before Mimi, his big hands laid loosely on his long, strong thighs.

Mimi took his hand—the one with scrapes and bruises on it—into hers. She felt dizzy with happiness. "Everything's all right with you and Lori?"

"Yes." He curved his long fingers around her hand. "Thanks to you we talked. God, I was so wrong about her. It never occurred to me that Melinda was lying to both of us. She turned me inside out in less than two years. She had more than sixteen years to work on Lori." He shuddered. "She told Lori I never sent money, never tried to see her. Then I showed up out of the clear blue on her sixteenth birthday and Lori let me have it. She didn't realize I'd spent years trying to find her."

"But now she does."

His smile tore at her heart.

"Yes. Now she does." He paused. "Kevin seems okay, too."

"They've had a hard time."

"Yeah." Dusty lifted her hand and pressed it against his throat. "Working, going to school, taking care of a baby. Yeah, they've had a hard time."

Mimi sensed his intent and began to smile. "But they won't now."

He smiled back. "No. Things are definitely looking up for the Kellys, financially and otherwise. But they'd have made it without me because they love each other. They really love each other and their baby."

"You find that hard to believe?"

"Not anymore. If *you* can love *me*, then anything is possible."

He reached into the chest pocket of his shirt and took out her engagement ring. Slowly and carefully he slipped it onto her finger. "Why do you love me, Mimi?" He spoke shyly, as if still trying to become comfortable with a new word and a new emotion.

She scrambled to her knees and faced him. He rose to meet her until they were thigh to thigh. She placed her hands upon his lean, creased cheeks, not even slowing to admire the diamond glittering on the third finger of her left hand. She'd have been equally thrilled with a cigar band. She looked into his eyes, willing him to believe her when she spoke from the heart.

"You're easy to love, Dustin McLain. You're as honest as a parson, honorable as a judge, and handsome as...as sin."

She was wrong, he thought—he was none of those things. He was just a man, but the luckiest man on earth, because the most wonderful woman on earth had fallen in love with him.

He shook his head, amazed not by her words but by the depth of his own feelings—feelings he no longer feared. He tried to pull her closer, but she held him off.

She smiled. "There are a million reasons why I love you and not one of them has a dollar sign in front of it."

And she smothered his explosive laughter with her lips.

# my VALENTINE 1992

Celebrate the most romantic day of the year with
MY VALENTINE 1992—a sexy new collection of four
romantic stories written by our famous Temptation
authors:

> GINA WILKINS
> KRISTINE ROLOFSON
> JOANN ROSS
> VICKI LEWIS THOMPSON

My Valentine 1992—an exquisite escape into a romantic
and sensuous world.

---

Don't miss these sexy stories, available in February at your favorite retail outlet. Or order your
copy now by sending your name, address, zip or postal code, along with a check or money
order for $4.99 (please do not send cash) plus 75¢ postage and handling ($1.00 in Canada),
payable to Harlequin Books to:

| In the U.S. | In Canada |
|---|---|
| 3010 Walden Avenue | P.O. Box 609 |
| P.O. Box 1396 | Fort Erie, Ontario |
| Buffalo, NY 14269-1396 | L2A 5X3 |

Please specify book title with your order.
Canadian residents add applicable federal and provincial taxes.

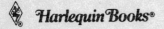

**Harlequin Books®**

VAL-92-R

# HARLEQUIN Temptation®

## Rebels & Rogues

All men are not created equal. Some are rough around the edges. Tough-minded but tenderhearted. Incredibly sexy. The tempting fulfillment of every woman's fantasy.

When it's time to fight for what they believe in, to win that special woman, our Rebels and Rogues are heroes at heart.

---

**Matt:** A hard man to forget . . . and an even harder man not to love.

**THE HOOD** by *Carin Rafferty*.
Temptation #381, February 1992.

**Cameron:** He came on a mission from light-years away . . . then a flesh-and-blood female changed everything.

**THE OUTSIDER** by *Barbara Delinsky*.
Temptation #385, March 1992.

---

At Temptation, 1992 is the Year of Rebels and Rogues. Look for twelve exciting stories, one each month, about bold and courageous men.

Don't miss upcoming books by your favorite authors, including Candace Schuler, JoAnn Ross and Janice Kaiser.

RR-2

# HARLEQUIN Temptation

## LOVE AND LAUGHTER

Look for: